Ghostly Theatre

The Festival Boss

Maureen Spurgeon

An Armada Original

For
Shirley and Ron, with love

The Festival Boss was first published in the UK
in Armada in 1989

Armada is an imprint of the Children's Division
part of the Collins Publishing Group,
8 Grafton Street, London W1X 3LA

Printed and bound in Great Britain by
William Collins Sons & Co. Ltd, Glasgow

One

"No!" shouted Scott's dad. "No, there isn't any more room on the roof rack! Anyone would think Studio Workshop was going to Melton Grange for ten months, not ten days."

"But it is the Youth Drama Festival, Dad," protested Tina. "You know, with proper make-up sessions, stage management classes, lessons on wardrobe and scenery — "

"Ending with a production put on by each group," finished Mr Melvin, tugging at the rope which held all the cases, boxes and cartons on top of his builder's van. "That's all we've been hearing about, ever since Lynsey booked it up."

"Just one last load of stuff, Dad,' Scott pleaded, clutching a box patched with brown paper and sticky tape. "I'm Studio Workshop's stage manager on this trip."

"And you want this up on the roof rack?" At least, thought Scott, his dad was smiling again. "You great twit! Come on, hand it over, and I'll put it by the front seat."

"Forget what time we said we'd pick up your mate Jason," grumbled Dad, glancing at his watch. "And he's a right Donny Daydreamer, always half an hour behind everyone else."

Oliver and Tina had to chuckle as they followed Scott into the van, piling on to the cushions and thick rugs Mrs Melvin had put inside. Donny Daydream — that just about summed up Jason.

But when the van turned into the High Street, there he was, waiting patiently outside his mum and dad's gift shop, a holdall at his feet, squinting through his steel-rimmed glasses in the wrong direction.

"Sound the horn, Dad!" cried Scott. "Hey, Jason! We're over here!"

"Good to see someone's on time," grinned Mr Melvin, getting out to open the van door. "Only Uncle Mike to collect now, and we're on our way."

"Seems funny not having Rachel with us," Jason remarked, looking around as if he half-expected her to be hiding somewhere. "Wonder why she went on the train with the others?"

"Because Lynsey wanted someone to help get everything sorted out for the drama festival!" Oliver explained, with a long-suffering sigh.

"It's a good thing we're all on half-term holiday at the same time," grinned Tina. "Anyone fancy a bag of crisps?"

"Lucky Dad and Uncle Mike are going right near Melton Grange, isn't it?" commented Scott, diving into the mammoth-size packet which Tina was holding out. "This is tons better than being on the train, rushing around to find seats together, then queuing up to get a drink."

This was enough to start the three boys talking about almost every train journey they could remember, and whether it was better to travel by road or rail.

Tina gazed out of the window, wondering what Rachel and Lynsey were doing at that moment. Probably scrambling for seats or queuing for a drink, the same as Scott said.

It was nice, having Scott and Oliver and Jason to herself, listening to their jokes and putting up with the way they liked to tease her. But Jason was right. It did feel strange without Rachel being there.

"You'll probably be sharing a room with Rachel!" said Scott, reading her thoughts.

"Seen the festival programme?" asked Oliver, pulling out a whole sheaf of papers. "There's something on nearly all the time."

"The Art of Mime... " Jason read out, looking over

Oliver's shoulder, "Music and Movement... Hey, there's even a session on making masks and wigs."

"Sounds fantastic," cried Tina, trying to get a look as well. "And what about Melton Grange?"

"One of the oldest boys' schools in the country," Uncle Mike broke in unexpectedly. "I wouldn't mind staying there, myself. All those lovely old rooms with the high ceilings, and big, log fires roaring way up the chimneys."

"It says here that the place is centrally heated," grinned Scott. "But I think you're right about everything else."

"You really love old places, don't you, Uncle Mike?" said Tina.

"Must do, to get your dad coming all this way to pick up some red bricks for Dreyton Manor! The place we're calling at was built at the same time as Melton Grange, I reckon. Shame it's near enough falling down, now."

"At least the red bricks will have a good home," Tina pointed out solemnly, "at Dreyton Manor."

Nobody spoke for a while, all of them thinking about the old manor house near their homes, half-ruined and forgotten for many years.

It was Rachel who had put them on the track of an old play called *The Merrie Devil of Dreyton*, ideal for Studio Workshop's part in the 400th Anniversary to celebrate Dreyton being granted a royal charter.

Not only had the production been a great success, the script had also led them to some valuable paintings, worth enough money for the manor to be rebuilt into a new arts centre.

"Should be able to get some of the doors and maybe a batch of window fittings, Mike," Scott's dad was saying as they drove along. "I'm hoping to make a start before the winter."

"And we're hoping to see the whole place finished," said Scott. "Then Studio Workshop can have a proper home at the arts centre."

"Lynsey never expected us to get into Dreyton Manor before next Easter," Oliver reminded him. "That's why the council gave us a special grant to take part in this Youth Drama Festival."

"And as a reward for finding those pictures of John Gabriel, the merrie devil blacksmith," added Jason in his deep-sounding voice. "There wouldn't have been any new arts centre at all without us."

This last remark of Jason's made them feel very happy. It was a lovely, clear day, more like August than mid-October, except for the occasional spatter of red and gold leaves as the van sped along.

Lulled by the steady hum of the engine and the warm weather, even Oliver found it the easiest thing in the world to drift into slumber, blissfully snoozing the miles away!

The next thing any of them knew was the van stopping with a jolt, waking them all up so suddenly, Tina and Jason were still blinking when the sound of marching music started blaring out.

"Someone turned up the radio?" asked Oliver, stretching his arms.

"Radio, nothing," snapped Scott's dad. "All the loud-speakers in the place must be going at full blast."

"What place?" murmured Jason, blinking again. "Is this Melton Grange?"

"Seems like it," Scott had to shout to make himself heard. "Stick your head out of the window and have a look."

Tina had already glimpsed a line of long, thin windows and wooden rafters through the trees, craning her neck to see a bit more of Melton Grange. From what Uncle Mike said, it sounded rather like their own Dreyton Manor, and she was looking forward to finding her way around.

"No sign of Lynsey or Rachel, is there?" Scott bawled out, as the van followed the drive around one side of the old building. "I thought they'd be here to meet us."

"Probably haven't arrived, yet," Oliver yelled back. "Maybe their train's late."

He was about to suggest finding the nearest entrance and asking for a hand with the luggage, when a loud voice boomed across the gravel path.

"Would you kindly get out of the way? You're interrupting our majorette routine!"

"Say that again?"

Scott could not blame Uncle Mike for looking annoyed. The woman seemed a real bossy-boots, acting as if none of them had any right to be there. Her short, pink-rinsed hair and shiny black practice outfit went well with her stern face, he thought.

"I said, you're interrupting our majorette routine. Why else do you suppose we have the music playing? None of the rehearsal rooms are available, so my students have to practice outdoors."

"But this is a driveway, lady," Mr Melvin pointed out. "You know? Where cars and vans drive along."

To prove his point, he revved up the engine – but the woman had turned her back and was clapping her hands in the air.

"Lead off from the left, Amanda. Everyone else, keep in step."

A flurry of tall, white bearskins, with matching skirts and jackets suddenly appeared from nowhere – so it seemed to Jason, blinking behind his glasses at the line of smiling, high-stepping girls marching out in front of the van.

"Well!" he burst out, as the last pair of white, sparkly boots disappeared around the side of the building. "D'you reckon we've come to the right place?"

"Of course we've come to the right place," cried Oliver. "Look who's up there, hanging out of the window to see

9

what all the row is about."

"Rachel!" yelled Tina, waving back at her friend. "And Lynsey!"

"Hi, you lot!" Dressed in her favourite shirt and dungarees, Lynsey looked more like Rachel's big sister than a drama coach. "Hello, Mr Melvin. We'll be right down."

"Thank goodness for that," Scott would not have been surprised to see his dad wiping his forehead with the back of his hand. "It's about time somebody told us what's going on here."

Two

"Don't take the Langham Theatre School too seriously," smiled Lynsey, helping to unload the luggage. "They only want to make a good impression."

"A good impression?" exploded Oliver. "Have you seen the woman in charge?"

"Betty Clark? Madame Helga, she calls herself now, but that wasn't her name when she was putting on concert parties, so I've heard. Her group's pretty good, though."

"Yes," Tina agreed in a small voice, remembering all the arms swinging in line, all the feet in perfect step. "Yes, anyone can see that."

"No need to sound so miserable about it!" grinned Rachel giving Tina a friendly shove. "Just wait till you see the rest of this place."

"OK if we unload the stuff here?" queried Scott's dad. "We've got our business to do, see."

"That's all right Mr Melvin, plenty of people around to lend a hand."

"If I might suggest, Madam," came a solemn-sounding voice, "the boxes and smaller cases can be carried in the service lift. The rest of the luggage can easily be sent up to your quarters later on. Wouldn't you agree?"

"Oh – er, yes," Lynsey was not used to being called "Madam", and she stepped back from the figure in the black jacket, high collar and pin-striped trousers with some respect. "Thanks, Fellowes."

"Fellowes does seem an old fogey," Rachel confided, as they followed her upstairs. "But it's only because he's the

11

janitor at Melton Grange school in term-time — you know, a bit stiff and starchy."

"Rachel," scolded Lynsey. She hoped Rachel's clear voice had not carried to the ground floor, where she could hear Fellowes giving orders to somebody. "I'm sure he's a very nice man."

"Never said he wasn't, did I?" Tina could tell that Rachel was pleased they were all together again, the way she was almost skipping up the stairs, stopping every so often to point things out.

"What about all those swords and shields and things on the walls? Pretty ancient, eh? And look at the old banners and flags hanging from the ceilings. How d'you like these old windows, Tina, with the little diamond panes?"

"They're lovely," Tina was glad to flop down on a low window-seat, worn smooth with age. She lifted a brass latch and pushed the window open, looking out into the walled garden below. "This reminds me of what Dreyton Manor must have been like."

"How do you know, when it was ruined before any of us were even born?" snorted Scott. "You're as bad as Uncle Mike."

There was so much to see at Melton Grange, Jason wondered how Lynsey and Rachel could find their way around so soon.

"You'll soon get used to being here, Jason," smiled Lynsey, seeing the look on his face.

"And at least you can't get locked in the library," added Rachel with a grin. "Or the chapel. They're both kept closed because of some sort of scare about all the valuable stuff that's here."

As Scott had predicted, Rachel and Tina were sharing a bedroom, right at the top of the grange, so that they could look out on to the roof.

"Fellowes says this was once the servants' quarters," Rachel enlightened them, "before Melton Grange became a school. Not bad, is it?"

"Where's our room, Ratchet?" asked Oliver, opening the door and poking his head outside. "Further along this landing?"

"Yes. You just go down those three steps, and it's the door right in front."

"Eh?" Jason seemed even more confused than usual. "Looks like a broom cupboard to me!"

He pulled the door open, and Tina gave a squeal, darting forward to stop an ancient-looking vacuum cleaner toppling over.

"It *is* a broom cupboard! You twit, Jason. Can't you see the door right beside it?"

The boys' room was quite a bit bigger than Rachel and Tina's, and it seemed to sprawl out into funny, odd-shaped corners, walls sloping down to the wooden floor, and a ceiling so low, Jason could almost reach up and touch it.

"This is great," pronounced Oliver, rubbing his hands with enthusiasm. "We must be right up under the roof."

"Probably," agreed Lynsey. "Now, before I forget, there's a buffet-disco arranged for tonight. It's to give all the drama groups at the festival a chance to meet each other."

"Hey, that sounds good," exclaimed Scott, grinning round at Jason and Oliver. "What time does it start?"

"Well," said Lynsey, "I know the dining hall's open at half past six. Hold on, and I'll check the rest of the details."

Lynsey stepped out on to the landing, almost bumping into Fellowes.

"Apologies for disturbing you, madam, but I wonder if the young gentlemen could kindly collect their hand luggage? Unfortunately, our service lift only goes up to the fourth floor."

"You'll find this way is the quickest," he continued, leading them along the landing towards a flight of narrow, wooden stairs, broken up every so often by steps which were broader and wider than the rest. There were a number of crooked little doors leading off the staircase, too, and Scott at once made up his mind to discover what was behind them.

"Here we are," Fellowes announced, pulling back the lift doors with a series of grinding squeaks. "Can you manage everything, or do you require help?"

"No, thanks," answered Oliver promptly, reaching out to grab the nearest case. He wanted to start nosing around, just as much as Scott did. "We'll be OK on our own."

"Where's the rest of the luggage?" asked Jason. But Fellowes had disappeared.

"Where did he go?" he wondered, turning his head this way and that, listening for footsteps on the stairs. "Don't tell me he just sort of melted away?"

"Sure, why not?" Scott grinned easily, pulling out the last of the bags. "He must know every inch of this place."

"Are you lot all right?" Rachel's voice floated down the stairs. "Lynsey's gone to check the fourth floor bedrooms."

"So we're the only ones right at the top?" demanded Oliver, sounding very pleased about it. "Brilliant!"

"The Langham Theatre School are on the third floor as well," said Tina, clattering down the last of the stairs. "They're still outside, rehearsing like mad."

Scott was about to add some other remark, when a loud crash resounded from the floor above, followed by the clatter of crockery crashing to the ground.

"Somebody's in our rooms!" yelled Oliver, going up the stairs two at a time, with Jason and Scott following close behind. "Hey, who's there? What's going on?"

There was quite a mess of broken china on the landing.

14

"You OK?" Rachel asked the girl in the plain black dress and white apron. "We thought somebody was trying to break in!"

"B-break in?" The girl was actually trembling, tucking every last wisp of hair inside her cap, shaking the whole time. "No... er, I was just bringing up a tray, and I — I tripped."

"Good thing it's lump sugar," said Tina, crouching down to refill the sugar basin.

Rachel thought the girl was about to burst into tears, and felt sorry for her. She didn't seem much older than they were.

"Doing this as a summer job, are you?" she enquired kindly. But the girl just scrabbled on the floor, biting her lip.

"Maybe the crash scared her," suggested Rachel after the girl had left, "and she thought everyone would come to see what happened, and she'd get into trouble."

"Come on, let's start unpacking," said Oliver impatiently, "otherwise we'll never make it to the buffet-disco."

But Lynsey made sure they were all ready in time. Wearing a pretty lacy blouse with a swirly skirt and sandals, Tina could not resist telling her how nice she looked.

"You look pretty good yourself, Tina. I could practically scream every time I see you and Scott with that fantastic red hair of yours."

"Shame I can't take mine off to lend you, Lynsey," Scott laughed, looking over the bannisters at everyone bustling into the big dining hall. "Hey, anyone notice the Langham Theatre School is right at the front again?"

"You needn't worry, Scotty," said Oliver with a grin. "We'll all make sure you don't go hungry."

"Any sign of that girl with the tray?" wondered Tina. But

it was impossible to tell who was there, with everyone milling around, carrying plates of pie and salad and sandwiches from the long buffet tables.

"This cheese flan is terrific," pronounced Oliver, taking a quick bite as the queue moved along. "Here, I'll take your plate and you can get us a couple of tubs of potato salad, Scotty. It's right there, in front of you."

"Right," said Scott, and reached out with both hands.

Whether somebody in front jerked back against him, or whether he was pushed from behind, Scott never knew. All he saw were two girls from the Langham Theatre School, grinning down at him, as he stumbled and fell to the floor.

"What happened, Scott?" asked Lynsey, hurrying towards him. "Was that your supper?"

"No, only some potato salad." Scott scowled up at the girls, but they had already turned their backs, helping themselves to the chicken drumsticks.

"Slip upstairs and get changed then."

Scott decided to take the service lift to the fourth floor, feeling very annoyed with himself. Fingering the wet splashes on his sweatshirt, he understood how the girl had felt when she dropped the tray.

It was very quiet when he came out of the lift – so quiet, that he actually tip-toed up the little wooden stairs. Then, at the end of the landing, he stopped, listening hard.

Somebody was in the boys' room. He could hear the wooden floorboards creaking softly, then, the rustle of things being shifted in a cupboard, or a drawer.

Slowly, he reached for the handle of the bedroom door, then drew his hand back again.

"The boss..." The words seemed to be swallowed up by the old walls of Melton Grange, almost as soon as they had been spoken. But Scott knew he was not mistaken.

"We've got to get to the boss."

16

Three

The low murmur of voices continued behind the door.

"But, where *is* the boss? Anyone know?"

Scott strained his ears, trying to catch what the answer was, but without success. Then came the voice again, rising with anger.

"We'll have to find out before long. Our only chance is to get to the boss while this drama festival is going on, or – "

But Scott had heard something else... the sound of footsteps on the landing, gradually getting louder, coming up right behind him.

"Hey!" somebody hissed. "What's up?"

"Jason!" Scott let out a deep breath. "Thank goodness it's you."

"Eh? Scotty, I only came to – "

"Someone's in our bedroom," whispered Scott, grabbing Jason's wrist. "Two of them, I reckon. Listen."

Together, they stood like two statues, waiting for the slightest sound to break the silence, their eyes fixed on the door.

"What about fetching Lynsey?" whispered Jason after a few minutes, but Scott shook his head impatiently. He wanted Jason with him when the door opened. Nobody could come out of the room as long as they were there.

Still the silence continued, it seemed for ages, until Jason could take no more.

"I'm going in," he whispered and turned the handle smartly. He felt for the light switch, looking around at the rather bare little room with its cream painted walls.

"No sign of anyone here, Scotty," he said at last. "Nothing at all."

"The window's open!" cried Scott, seeing the curtains fluttering in the cold night air. "Maybe that's how they got away."

"So how did they manage to turn round and close the window behind them? It's only open a couple of inches."

Scott was beginning to feel a bit stupid. The window was the sort which had to be pushed up and pulled down, and Jason was having quite a job to lift it high enough to look out into the grounds.

"I can't see anyone getting out of the room before we came in, Scotty. Not if you said you just heard them talking in here!"

"But, I *did* hear them talking," Scott protested. "Why else d'you think I was standing outside with my shirt all mucked up? I tell you, they were going on about their boss, saying they'd have to find him while the festival was going on."

Jason closed the window. Something had bothered Scott, he was sure of that. But, he reasoned, why should anyone want to nose around their bedroom?

"Is all our stuff still here?" he asked suddenly, waiting for Scott to put on another sweatshirt. "Anything taken? I mean, none of the drawers are pulled out, or anything."

"No..." Scott clutched his mop of red hair in confusion, recalling the strange sounds he had heard. "No, everything looks the same. And don't say they can't have vanished into thin air. I *know* somebody was in here, and I know I heard them talking."

"I'm not saying you didn't," said Jason mildly. "But maybe it was somebody in another room, that man Fellowes, or someone."

Scott's freckled face cleared a little.

"Suppose that could be it," he conceded. "We all thought Fellowes did a good disappearing act on the landing earlier on, remember?"

"Sure." That still didn't explain about the boss Scott had heard being mentioned, but Jason felt he'd had enough brain-teasers for one evening. "Now, are you ready for the disco? Ollie sent me up to fetch the camera."

"It's in the locker beside my bed, the one with all the stage gear inside. I'll get it."

The buffet was still in progress when they got back to the party, but now there was plenty going on at the other end of the hall as well.

Turntables and speakers had been set up on a portable stage, and two young men in black trousers and white shirts were putting the finishing touches to an impressive array of decorations and coloured lights.

"You might have picked up a few tips on the sound system if you'd been down here a bit sooner," Oliver informed Scott through mouthfuls of cold sausage. "What was the hold-up?"

"Tell you about it later on," promised Scott, wanting to get on with the cheese flan and the long-awaited potato salad.

"Clear the floor, all you dancers," one of the disc jockeys announced into the microphone, fading the music at the same time. "Find yourself a partner from one of the other groups. First couple back on the floor wins a prize!"

"Th-that girl," gasped Scott, backing away hurriedly. "Amanda, isn't it? The one who was leading the tap dance routine? Oh, no... Don't say — "

"She's heading straight towards you, Scotty," grinned Oliver, giving him a nudge. "Must be something to do with that hair of yours."

Scott barely had time to put his plate down before

Amanda pulled him across to the dance floor, ready to be presented with a packet of chocolate creams amid cheers from the Langham girls.

"Load of rubbish," he scowled.

"What about handing over your chocolates, then?" Amanda taunted him. "Put those in your pocket quick enough, didn't you?"

"Well, he did miss a helping of potato salad, Mandy," another girl chimed in, gratified to see Scott's face darken in a fresh wave of scowls.

"Now, look," Scott began angrily, and they all laughed out loud. With the music fading again, everyone could hear his retort at the other end of the hall.

"New partners, please."

"Brilliant," snarled Scott, and stamped off to find Rachel. But the combination of long, fair hair and blue eyes had already attracted another partner, with "PICTON YOUTH DRAMA" on his T-shirt. And one of the Langham boys was leading Tina on to the floor.

"Lynsey," Scott called out — just as she was being whisked away by Oliver. Even Jason had been drawn into the thick of the dancing.

"Definitely not my night!" he growled under his breath, and reached out for his plate which he'd been forced to abandon minutes before. The flan and potato salad still looked appetizing enough, so he picked up his plastic fork, trying to cheer up.

He had hardly turned round and swallowed the first mouthful, when there was a crash right behind him, loud enough to make the whole table judder against him.

"Flaming heck," Scott burst out before he could stop himself. "Seems I won't get the chance to eat anything until tomorrow's breakfast."

Glancing around at the black dress and white apron, he

thought at first it was the girl with the tray. Then he saw that the woman was much older.

"Sorry, love. My fault for trying to stack too many plates at once. More haste, less speed, my mother always said."

She spoke so gently that Scott wished he had held his tongue. The woman seemed to sense this, pushing a dish of pickled eggs towards him.

"Go on, help yourself, lad. And I've got some homemade apple tart under the counter if you fancy a piece."

For the first time that evening, Scott's face creased into a warm smile.

"Terrific party, wasn't it?" sighed Rachel, flopping down at the edge of her bed and pulling off a pale green sneaker shoe. "Let's finish unpacking tomorrow, shall we?"

"Right." Tina went to the huge chest of drawers which stood in one corner of their bedroom. "And we'll dump today's clothes in the bottom drawer, out of the way."

Rachel smiled to herself, stretching lazily on the bed and listening to the boys moving around in their room.

"Rachel..." Tina's voice made her sit up with a start. "Rachel, look what was in the drawer. It was the name Melton Grange that made me notice..."

She held out a sheet of newspaper which had been folded to line the inside of the drawer, pointing to a headline for Rachel to read.

Melton Grange Robbery
Burford Police confirmed yesterday that despite full-scale enquiries, no further progress has been made regarding the theft of the Lady Elizabeth gold chalice from the chapel of Melton Grange Boys' School last week. Full Story, page 3.

Four

"There's definitely something going on here," pronounced Oliver, his brown eyes glued to the report in the *Burford Echo*. "You sure page three isn't anywhere in your room, Ratchet?"

"Ask me that question once more, Oliver Davis..." said Rachel between her teeth. "We were searching half the night, Tina and me."

"We pulled out every single drawer, and read through every sheet of paper," added Tina.

"Don't let's argue," Jason broke in wearily. He glanced at Scott. "There's something we've got to tell you. Right, Scotty?"

So Scott told them about the voices he had heard, the sound of things being moved around inside the room, and everything that was said about the mysterious boss.

"But when we went in, there wasn't anyone here. And nobody came out of the room, either."

"The window was open," said Jason, "but not wide enough for anyone to get through."

"But there might be a balcony or a ledge right underneath," Oliver suggested, trying to look out. "Something to step on, then pull the window down a bit. Wonder how we can check?"

"Hang something out of the window," Jason replied promptly. "Something we could see from outside. What about Scotty's mucky sweatshirt?"

"I'd like to know what's so important about this boss, and why he's got to be tracked down before the festival ends," declared Rachel. "Sounds as if he could be the boss of a gang that's tied up with the robbery, doesn't it?"

"But, why were they up here in the first place?" Scott demanded helplessly.

Nobody could think of an answer to that one. Besides, they were all soon busy helping Jason to pull the window down on the waistband of the sweatshirt, leaving the rest hanging outside.

They barely had time to get their breath back, before the shrill call of an electric bell rang through the building.

"Breakfast!" Scott yelled, and made for the door.

Halfway through the cornflakes and poached eggs on toast, a youngish man in a faded tracksuit jumped up on to the platform.

"That's John Turner," Lynsey enlightened them. "He's the festival organizer."

"The boss," said Jason, with a meaningful glance at Scott.

"The boss?" Lynsey gave a little laugh. "Yes, if you like, Jason."

But John Turner didn't look much like a gangland boss, Tina considered. True, he was tall and beefy, with broad shoulders and a square jaw. But his long hair and round glasses gave him a humourous look, which went well with the breezy way he spoke.

"OK, carry on eating while I tell you what's going on. We start this morning with a session on improvisation to music. Then, for this afternoon, there's the choice of a cinema presentation, or a tour of the library and school chapel."

"Hear that?" hissed Oliver across the table. "We can see around the chapel after dinner."

"Really, Oliver?" They could hear that Lynsey sounded surprised. "What's so special about that?"

"Well, this could be the only chance we get," Rachel

broke in hastily. "Hasn't it been closed for a while, Lynsey?"

"Yes..." Lynsey poured out some more coffee. "This afternoon's tour must have been included in the festival programme before the robbery."

"The robbery?" echoed Scott innocently. "Has there been a robbery, then?"

"Yes," said Lynsey again. "A gold chalice was stolen. And don't you dare start asking questions, understand? Fellowes practically bit John's head off yesterday when he happened to mention it."

"Well, the chalice must have been valuable," said Oliver, sounding very wise. He wanted to keep Lynsey talking.

"Yes, it was. But whenever the subject crops up, there's this cold, frosty silence, as if there's some terrible secret. It's enough to get on people's nerves."

"I'll put your names down, anyway," she continued briskly. "The younger ones will probably prefer the film."

The scraping of chair legs on the floor and sounds of the tables being cleared signalled the end of breakfast, and Lynsey glanced up at the big clock on the wall.

"Hey, we've got about ten minutes before the morning session starts in the Great Hall. Best get a move on, you lot!"

The Great Hall was quite a place to be in, Oliver decided, looking around at the collection of old weapons and shields displayed on the walls. Narrow windows reached up towards the wooden beams which stretched across the ceiling, and threads of pale sunshine sprinkled on the rounded wooden plates which kept the swords in place, spreading out like the petals of a spiky flower.

But it was the grand stage which impressed everyone. It took up one end of the Great Hall, with a line of footlights tilted towards the blue velvet backcloth, and a splendid set

24

of matching side curtains, pulled back for John Turner to take centre stage.

"Now, you're all going to hear a popular piece of music," he was saying. "After that, each group will go into a room on their own to work out a short improvisation, using the music either to set the scene or provide a background for the piece. He pressed a switch on a large tapedeck.

> *"Oh, I do like to be be-side the sea-side!*
> *Oh, I do like to be be-side the sea...."*

The audience looked around at each other and there were quite a few sniggers. It was amazing how embarrassing it felt, standing and listening to a sing-along record!

"Not much of a theme, I don't think," said Jason gloomily. "It's always started raining when I've been to the seaside. The sea's usually freezing, and — "

"Hold on," Oliver interrupted, frowning in concentration. "What about a family on the beach, with everyone getting changed, ready for a swim or a paddle. Only, like Jason says, the sea's freezing cold."

"So they'd run in, then out again." Scott could see it all in his mind. "Then it starts raining, so they rush to get dressed, grabbing all their things, getting in a right state... "

"And they just have to sit, wishing the rain would stop." finished Rachel.

"Have to be a big family to get all of us in," commented Suzy, perched on one of the desks. "Couldn't we make it an outing, instead?"

"That'd be tons better," agreed Robert, keen to see everyone with a good part to play. "What about it, Oliver?"

The idea took shape quickly. Jason and Rachel, being the tallest, were in charge of the outing, with Robert leading the swimmers, Tina looking after the paddlers, and Oliver

25

organizing a beach picnic despite the rain. Scott was the camera-man, trying to make them all smile to the bitter end!

When the practice time was up, all the groups went back into the Great Hall, ready to perform on stage.

Picton Youth Drama had worked out a clever puppet routine which very much appealed to Tina's sense of rhythm and dance. Another group called Mainline Players chose a fairground as their theme, with horses on a roundabout and a coconut shy.

And, although the Elmfield Drama Club came close to Studio Workshop's idea with their comic presentation of a disastrous boat trip which made everyone seasick, the proud smile on Lynsey's face when the last make-believe photograph had been taken told them they had done well.

"An original, amusing theme, very well put together," was John Turner's verdict. "You made the audience really laugh, and I'd certainly like to see a repeat performance."

"Quite a compliment," Lynsey grinned. "Now, let's see what the Langham Theatre School have done."

Madame Helga had seen to it that the reputation of her group had already got round, so there was an expectant hush as the curtains were swept back with a flourish.

A line of chorus girls high-kicked their way from one side of the stage, all moving in perfect rhythm, perfect formation. One by one came the jugglers, the acrobats, the clowns, the balancing acts, the musicians, finally coming together for the farewell number. But after a cheery goodbye, there was only a bent, old man, sweeping the stage alone.

The cheering and applause began almost before the music had ended.

"Magic!" shouted Tina. "Real magic!"

Before the applause had finished, Tina left the hall for a

bit of fresh air. She still felt tired from the previous night, what with finding the newspaper, then hunting around with Rachel, and talking about the robbery.

She thought about the boss Scott had heard somebody talking about — somebody who wasn't in the room when he and Jason came in, yet couldn't have gone out through the door.

Could they have squeezed through the window, somehow, and dropped down on to a ledge, like Oliver was saying?

Tina lifted her head towards the tall chimneys of Melton Grange, her eyes searching for the sweatshirt hanging outside.

Finding it proved to be quite difficult. There seemed to be windows everywhere she looked, and her neck soon began to ache. So she started walking all around the outside of Melton Grange, raising her eyes every so often.

She was just coming towards the corner of the fourth wall when she saw it. It looked so small and funny, with the sleeves drooping down over the window sill, and flopping against the flat wall. No ledge or balcony there.

Something else caught her eye. At first she thought it might be the reflection of the sweatshirt in the window pane. If she had glanced away for only a second, she would have told herself it was imagination. Only it wasn't.

Somebody was in the boys' bedroom again, moving around, trying to find something. Somebody with red hair, the same as hers and Scott's.

And Tina knew she just had to find out who it was!

Five

It was very quiet inside Melton Grange, not a soul in sight. Tina only had to slip behind the front desk and take the key from the row of hooks on the wall...

"May I help you, young lady?"

She would never have known Fellowes was there.

"I — I only wanted the key to my brother's room."

"Quite. I take it that the morning session finished earlier than expected?"

"N — no..." Tina stammered again. "But, I — I remembered I'd left something in Scott's room. Can I take the service lift?"

"You may. And in future, if you require a key, perhaps you could remember to ask me."

"Yes. Sorry, Mr Fellowes."

Her heart was thumping as she stepped out of the lift and crept up the short flight of stairs.

That was when she knew for certain that there definitely was someone in the boys' room.

"The boss..." Her ears were every bit as sharp as Scott's. "How do we find the boss?"

A series of dull thuds muffled the next part of the conversation, and Tina heard no more. She held her breath, leaning back against the wall.

Then there were footsteps, and the door handle turning slowly... the door slowly opening...

Tina gave such a loud sigh of relief that the girl turned round sharply, wiping her hands down the front of her flowered overalls.

"Just finishing this room, miss," she burst out, tucking her hair underneath a head-scarf, the same as she had when Tina saw her the first time, picking up tea-cups and a sugar bowl. "Did you want something?"

"Is my brother here?" Why was the girl keeping her at the door, she wondered? What was wrong? "I thought I saw him at the window."

"The window?" Tina could tell the girl was flustered, the way she started to blush bright red, her eyebrows standing out like thick sooty-black ridges. "I'm the only one here, miss. It must've been me that you saw."

"Oh, well..." Tina knew she had to think quickly. "I – I'll take his sweatshirt, then."

"Sweatshirt, miss?"

"We had to hang it out of the window to dry off. He spilt some potato salad down the front."

"Oh, I see." The girl gave a nervous little laugh, and glanced back into the room. "Suppose I wash it out and bring it in tomorrow, how's that?"

"Thanks," Tina had to smile back at the girl, she seemed so pleased to help. "My name's Tina. What's yours?"

"Kate..." She flushed again, hastily stuffing a duster into her overall pocket. "Well, I'd best be getting on with my work, then."

"Yes..." Tina fiddled with the key in her hand, staring hard at the closed door. Could there be somebody else in there, she wondered, somebody with red hair? Or had she been mistaken, after all?

"Might I enquire," came the solemn-sounding voice of Fellowes, "if you found what you required in your brother's room?" Once again, the black jacket and pin-striped trousers seemed to appear from nowhere.

"Yes," Tina replied hastily, then she saw he'd noticed her empty hands as she handed back the key. "I – I mean, no. That is, Scott must have taken it."

"Really?" Fellowes didn't sound as if he believed her. "Then perhaps you'd care to rejoin your party in good time for lunch. The morning session is now over."

He led the way downstairs without another word, and pushed the button for the service lift. The silence between them was so tense, so cold, it seemed to take ages to reach the ground floor.

"Rachel!" Tina felt she had never been so glad to wave to her friend in her whole life. "Rachel!"

"Tina! Hey, Tina, where did you get to? We were looking all over the place for you!"

She slipped her arm through Tina's, looking anxiously at the troubled expression on the younger girl's face. "So, what happened to you?"

"Wait until the boys are here," Tina said. "Then I'll tell you."

Tina's account of a red-haired stranger in the room and another mention of the unknown boss certainly added a lot of interest to a lunch of shepherd's pie and peas. But she couldn't help being disappointed that nobody quite knew what to do next.

"We might have known the cleaners would need a set of keys," said Oliver, glad of all the chatter around him. "You say someone else could have been hiding in the room, Tina?"

"Well," said Tina after some thought, "it wasn't Kate I saw at the window. She hasn't got red hair, and she didn't notice the sweatshirt hanging outside, either."

"Wouldn't hurt to give our room a good going-over," added Jason. "Search under the beds, behind the wardrobes – everywhere. Even if we don't find anywhere a person could hide, there might be something they've left behind."

"We'll have to do that later," said Oliver. "Right now it's

30

the tour of the chapel and the library, and we can't miss that."

"Hope you enjoy yourselves!" cried Lynsey, conducting the rest of Studio Workshop towards the film room. "Doctor Julian Cole, the history master from Melton Grange is going to show you around, so have a good time."

"Oh, no!" groaned Jason, seeing a familiar figure standing by the front desk, where they had been told to wait. "Don't say *she's* tagging along, as well."

"Madame Helga," exclaimed Scott. "I wouldn't put it past Langham to get us lumbered with her."

"Well, at least they're not here," Oliver reminded him. "There can't be many seats left for the film."

"Maybe that was the general idea," Jason suggested. "It could be a bit dodgy, having a load of people going round the chapel after the robbery."

"Belt up, Jason," Scott snapped, seeing two members of the Elmfield Drama Group coming up to join them. "D'you want to get us kicked out before we even start?"

But Jason couldn't see that happening. Without the five of them, there would have been only three visitors being ushered into the cramped, rather gloomy surroundings of the dimly-lit chapel. And Doctor Cole did seem to enjoy having an audience.

"It was meant to be a family chapel," he explained, waving a hand around the bare walls. "So there would only be a small number of people using it."

"It's very plain," remarked Madame Helga, patting the beads around her neck. She viewed the hard wooden seats and the bare floorboards with some distaste, clearly preferring everything to shine and sparkle. "No stained glass windows, no ornaments, pictures or anything."

"The chapel dates from the time of Oliver Cromwell," Dr Cole informed her. "And he strongly disapproved of all

31

unnecessary trimmings."

"You mean, this is all there is here?" asked Rachel, eagerly backing up Madame Helga. "Nothing else?"

There was a polite cough from the back of the chapel, and Scott saw Oliver and Jason glancing warily at each other.

Fellowes had been there the whole time, listening to every word.

"The school does have a few treasures which are used in the chapel," said Doctor Cole slowly. "But only on very special occasions."

"But aren't they ever on show?" persisted Scott. "Can't we see them?"

"I'm afraid not. Now, if you would like to look up at the ceiling – "

"What's the point of showing people around a place when we can't see the most important things in it?" demanded Madame Helga. "And it's quite ridiculous that you refuse to tell us anything at all about them."

"I appreciate your disappointment, madam," the solemn tones of Fellowes echoed around the bare walls. "All I can tell you is that we have very serious reasons for saying as little as possible about the items normally kept in the chapel. I am sure you will understand."

From the disgruntled look on Madame Helga's face, it was quite clear she did not understand. But before she could protest again Doctor Cole was opening the chapel door, ready to lead them all out into the corridor.

"The library is just along here," he announced brightly, as if, Oliver thought, he was glad to leave Fellowes locking the chapel door behind him, keys jangling noisily.

The library was a pleasant surprise. As well as the shelves and shelves of books, there were glass cases with old coins, diaries, whole collections of picture cards, butterflies and pressed flowers — even a set of tinder-boxes.

Like the Great Hall, weapons and swords were displayed on the walls, as well as two complete suits of armour standing either side of an enormous fireplace, big enough for Scott to stand inside.

"The very spot where some chimney-sweep boy stood, many years ago," said Doctor Cole, "before he started his long climb up into the chimney. I daresay he left plenty of soot behind, too."

"And weren't there supposed to be all sorts of nooks and crannies for people to hide?" asked Madame Helga, appearing very knowledgeable. "One hears so many stories about priests hiding inside chimneys."

"Quite right!" Doctor Cole smiled again. "But, we haven't found any priests' hidey-holes at Melton Grange so far."

The rest of the afternoon passed so quickly, none of them could believe it when the bell went. Even putting up with Madame Helga hadn't been so bad.

"I thought she was great, the way she kept on at Fellowes and Doctor Cole," Rachel admitted. "Shame we didn't find out anything about the chalice, though."

"I was thinking of going down to the offices of the *Burford Echo*," said Oliver thoughtfully. "The address must be somewhere in that newspaper Tina found."

"Let's look up the address in the phone book, while we're down here," suggested Scott, and began to feel in his pockets. "I think I've got a pen in my wallet..."

"I bet you left it behind," said Oliver, watching Scott's search become more frantic by the minute.

"No, I didn't!" Scott was getting annoyed now, but the others were already hurrying up the stairs, wanting to get the address of the *Burford Echo* without waiting any longer.

"Nothing like having friends, is there?" he growled to himself, dashing back to the library.

Suppose the door was locked, he thought, gripping the cold handle. Suppose there was nobody else to open the door? Suppose...

The door opened so easily, Scott had to chuckle to himself. And, yes – there was his wallet, right at the edge of the fireplace.

"So, you're back again," growled a deep voice, and Scott heard the sudden swish of all the blinds coming down at once, plunging the room into darkness.

"You'd better be listening, kid." Somebody came up from behind, grabbing Scott with one massive hand, the other coming down hard over his mouth. "Because this is your last chance! Understand?"

Desperately, Scott tried to struggle free, but the grip of iron only held him tighter.

"Just in case you need reminding, you're meant to be away from here. And unless it's right away this time, there'll be trouble. I'm warning you..."

Six

"Now, listen!" the man barked in Scott's ear. "If we see you hanging anywhere around here again, you'll be sorry. You're in enough trouble as it is."

Scott tried desperately to break free, wriggling as hard as he could, kicking out blindly in the dark. But he knew it was no good. The powerful grip only tightened still more.

"Right!" came the voice again, releasing Scott with a vicious shove. "You're going to wait here until it's nice and quiet. Then you can go back where you came from. And no funny business, trying to be too clever, get it?"

Scott was much too scared to argue. There were no more voices, no further sounds. But the room was still pitch black, too dark for him to see anything.

He let out a deep, shuddering breath, trying to think clearly.

"You're meant to be away from here... You're in enough trouble... You'll be sorry..."

The words still echoed in his ears, he could hear them repeating and repeating, over and over again, until it made him dizzy.

"Scott! Scott..."

It felt like somebody was calling him from the edge of a thick, black whirlpool, with him spinning round and round, down and down.

"Scott! Scott..."

"He only went to get his wallet, Lynsey. He must be around, somewhere."

"Let's hope so, Oliver. The sooner Fellowes puts my mind at rest, the better."

There was the clang of a key in the lock, and the door creaked open. Only a little light spilled in from the corridor outside — but that was enough to see Scott, sprawled out on the floor, at the feet of a suit of armour.

"Scott! Oh, Scott, what's happened?"

Rachel was relieved to see him stirring at the sound of Lynsey's voice, his face unusually pale underneath the mass of red hair.

"My — my head..." he moaned, raising a hand to his forehead. "I must've fallen..."

"Indeed," observed Fellowes, cold as ever. "Why did you not come to me when you suspected that you had left your property in here? I've already had to speak to your sister, and now — "

"Yes, all right. Mr Fellowes," Lynsey interrupted quickly. "Oliver, Jason, can you help me get Scott upstairs? He doesn't seem badly hurt."

"There was somebody in the library," Scott rambled on, clutching his aching head. "Somebody grabbed hold of me in the library..."

"The boy has obviously been affected by the accident," murmured Fellowes. "Perhaps it might be as well to send him home."

"Send him home?" Oliver echoed in horror. "But Studio Workshop couldn't be in the drama festival without Scott!"

"I agree it is most unfortunate. But I do think you should consider — "

"Thanks for the advice, Mr Fellowes," Lynsey interrupted again. "You'll be glad to know I've had a First Aid Nursing Certificate since I started Studio Workshop three years ago. I'll ask for a doctor if it's necessary."

"Don't need a doctor..." mumbled Scott, gingerly

feeling the bump on his forehead. "I fell over in the dark, that's all."

"Serves you right for getting yourself locked in," said Lynsey, sounding almost as unfeeling as Fellowes. Then she gave one of her laughs.

"It's all right, I know you didn't mean to cause all this fuss, Scott. Come along, let's see what the damage is."

Scott quite enjoyed being the centre of attention.

"Nothing more than a bump on the head with a graze to go with it," pronounced Lynsey at last. "But it's going to feel a bit sore for a while. How do you feel about having a quiet evening, just for once?"

Scott nodded weakly, allowing himself to be led towards his bed.

"Oliver and Jason can keep you company, while we nip downstairs to give Fellowes the good news, and arrange for something to eat. OK?"

"Can you bring me a cola?" croaked Scott, but Lynsey pretended she hadn't heard.

"He'll be as right as rain by tomorrow," they heard her telling Rachel and Tina. "Nothing that a strip of plaster and a dab of iodine won't put right."

"That's a break," breathed Oliver thankfully. "You could've got us kicked out of the festival, Scotty."

"What about me?" Scott sat up sharply, quite forgetting the bump on his head. "A whole gang set on me in the library. Jumped on me from behind, they did, then a hand came over my mouth, and they said that if I didn't – "

"How many of them were there?" asked Jason calmly. "Three? Four? A dozen?"

"Well..." Scott tried to think. "I only heard one man's voice, the one who grabbed me just as I picked up my wallet." He patted his back pocket to make sure, trying to get everything straight in his mind. "Only it didn't seem like he was on his own: 'You'd better be listening, kid! Just in case you need reminding, you're meant to be away from here...'"

Scott was a born impersonator, able to mimic the man's gruff tones almost perfectly. It was enough to convince Oliver and Jason that he was telling the truth.

"And then it all went quiet, and I – well, I must have crashed into something and banged my head," he ended lamely. "It was too dark to see anything."

"But you only went back to look for your wallet," Oliver pointed out at last. "Surely that doesn't call for the tough-guy act."

"Reckon we ought to tell Lynsey?" asked Jason.

"What? You heard what old Fellowes said when Scotty tried telling him. If Lynsey puts in a complaint or anything, you can bet he'd really make trouble for all of us."

"You're right," Scott agreed, lying back on his pillow. "Wanted me sent home quick enough, didn't he? Sounds like a good mate of that fella in the library."

None of them said anything for quite a few moments. Then Oliver spoke again, putting into words what all three of them were thinking.

"There's something behind all this, something we don't know about. Why should anyone pick on Scott for no reason at all?" He paused. "Know what I think?"

"What?" said Jason and Scott, both together.

"They thought he was somebody else!"

Jason gave a low whistle. "You mean they picked on the wrong person? It was all a mistake?"

"I reckon so. The thing is, who is he, this other boy? Where is he now? What's he done? We'll have to find out before Scotty gets picked on again."

"Thanks a bunch, Ollie!" Scott retorted tartly. "That's made me feel a whole lot better."

"No sense in taking chances, is there?" Oliver was too sensible to let Scott's outburst worry him. "So, from now on, us three keep together. OK, Scotty?"

Scott merely shrugged his shoulders and laid back on the pillow. He knew when he was beaten.

"And don't let's say anything to the girls," added Oliver in a whisper, hearing Rachel and Tina on the landing. "All right!" he called out. "Hold on, you two, I'm opening the door."

"What is it we're not supposed to know?" asked Tina, edging into the room with a tray of sandwiches, apples, bananas and chocolate cup cakes.

"Er, we were only talking about the stolen chalice," Jason burst out, saying the first thing that came into his head. "You know... a gang of thieves with that boss in charge. Ollie wanted to call in at the newspaper offices tomorrow, remember?"

"And I suppose that means you don't want us tagging along?" demanded Rachel.

"We haven't even looked up the address, yet," said Oliver calmly, taking the tray and setting it down on the dressing table. "Hey, how come you got all this, Ratchet?"

"That lady who was at the disco. You know, the one we saw piling up Scott's plate every five minutes." Rachel had to chuckle at the memory. "She must think you're a right weakling, Scotty!"

"I feel like one, right now," confessed Scott, managing to reach out for a salmon sandwich and a tomato. "Nice having our eats up here, isn't it, just the five of us?"

"What were you saying about going to the Burford Gazette without us." said Rachel. Oliver glanced quickly at Jason. As long as she thought that's what they had been talking about before she and Tina came into the room, they would be saved any more awkward questions.

"Suppose it would look a bit suspicious, all of us turning up just for one paper," she admitted, twiddling with her drinking straw. "Isn't the address you want on the page we found, Ollie? I put it in Scott's cabinet, underneath the camera."

It took a good half hour of careful searching before they got the address of the *Burford Echo* — and, then it was right at the bottom of the back sports page, which Tina discovered lining the waste-paper basket.

"The Bridgestone Press!" she cried triumphantly. "25, Chapel Street, Burford! Anyone know where that is?"

"I bet Scott's tea-lady can soon tell us," said Oliver. "We'll say we want to find our way around the town, that's the truth, anyway. There's bound to be a map around, somewhere."

"Trouble is," broke in Jason, polishing his glasses so that he could read one of the programmes for the drama festival, "we don't have much time to ourselves until Wednesday. And then Lynsey was talking about doing some rehearsals."

"We've just got to make it tomorrow, somehow," declared Oliver, almost snatching the programme from Jason. "What's the first session?"

"Wardrobe and costumes," supplied Tina eagerly. This was one of her favourite subjects, and she was already looking forward to it. "Then there's some demonstrations on make-up."

"You're not thinking of getting down to the newspaper office and back before the session starts, are you, Ollie?" demanded Jason. "You'd never make it, not even if the place was only round the corner!"

"I've got a better idea than that," scoffed Oliver, looking pleased with himself. "We'll be calling at the *Burford Echo* in the morning, Scotty and me, I've worked it all out.

There's just one thing – "

He stopped, raising a finger to his lips. The others had heard it, too, the sudden creaking of floorboards outside.

Everyone held their breath, watching Oliver creeping across the room, his fingers slowly closing around the handle, turning it as quietly as he could.

The door opened much too loudly, and too quickly, but that hardly mattered. He was still able to see the back view of a plump figure hurrying towards the stairs, rings and beads gleaming softly in the mellow light as she reached out a hand to steady herself.

"What's she doing up here?" muttered Oliver, half under his breath. "It – it's Madame Helga!"

Seven

Madame Helga, or no Madame Helga — Oliver was determined to see his plan through.

"What can she do, anyway?" he demanded, more than once. "Nothing!"

But the others weren't so sure.

"I thought it was funny, her being with us on the library tour, asking all those questions." Scott kept saying. "And she can't have been listening at the door for nothing."

"Might not have been listening at the door," said Tina, trying to be fair. "Maybe she was looking for somebody — Lynsey, perhaps."

"Maybe she's just plain nosey," suggested Jason bluntly. "Wanting to find out what happened to Scott, and why we weren't in the dining hall last night."

"Why didn't she just knock at the door and ask, then?" Rachel cut in, but Oliver's quick mind had already moved on.

"Reckon you can all cover up for Scotty and me while we're down at the *Burford Echo*? It shouldn't be too much bother."

"Why does Scott have to go with you?" Tina wanted to know. "Lynsey's sure to notice!"

"No, she won't," Oliver insisted testily. "It's a session on costume this morning, OK? So how is she going to check, with everyone getting into their gear at the same time?"

' "We'll be back before you know it!" added Scott, trying to make Tina feel better about the whole idea. "Mabel the tea lady says Chapel Street isn't too far, just down the hill and along the road, that's all."

"Now, don't forget, Jason," Oliver continued, lowering his voice because John Turner was taking the stage in the Great Hall, "tag on to Robert as soon as he's in costume! He's about my size…"

"Quiet, please," called John Turner, and clapped his hands. He prided himself on being very prompt when it came to starting at the proper time. "Now, we all know that wardrobe is very important in drama, but most of us do not use it nearly enough!"

He called two people up on to the stage – Amanda from the Langham Theatre Group, and Rory from Picton Youth Drama. He gave them one piece of costume each – a plain nightdress for Amanda and a jacket for Rory – and gave them a startling demonstration.

The nightdress became a sari, a milkmaid's smock, Bo-Peep's dress, a Victorian wedding outfit. Wearing the jacket tied with string, Rory was a poor tramp, soon to be transformed into a handsome bridegroom with the addition of a bow tie and a flower in the buttonhole.

A murmur of admiration ran through the Great Hall, swelling into a burst of enthusiastic applause. John Turner looked very pleased.

"Your drama teachers have seen to it that the costumes for your own productions at the drama festival have been sent down to the lobby of the Great Hall," he announced. "What I'd like you to do is to use those costumes to make two different crowd scenes."

"Great!" exclaimed Oliver, as everyone scurried around, finding the right boxes, or – in the case of the Langham Theatre Group – two splendid hampers bulging with sequins and shiny satins. "We're on our way, Scotty."

"Hope somebody's got some bright ideas!" said Daniel, the earnest-looking boy who was Squire Melrose in their play, *The Merrie Devil of Dreyton*. He held up a pair of knee-length trousers with some dismay. "Can't see what I could use these for, except the old-fashioned breeches they're meant to be."

"Oh, borrow Ollie's blacksmith belt with the big buckle and be a pirate!" Rachel snapped unexpectedly. Tina wondered if the thought of Oliver and Scott's trip into town was making her nervous. "We can all wear scarves and things around our heads and over one eye, that kind of thing, can't we?"

"Good old Ratchet," Oliver muttered in Scott's direction. "Come on, let's get going."

It was so easy, Scott felt sure that something had to go wrong. Only it didn't.

They set off at a run, glancing back once or twice to see if anyone had seen them leaving Melton Grange. But it seemed nobody was interested in two figures wearing jackets which might have been windcheaters, and trousers which could have been track-suit bottoms tucked into thick socks.

"Cross country runners, out training," a man told his dog, seeing Oliver and Scott jogging along down the hill.

"Must be a football match somewhere, today," said a lady in a telephone box. "Two supporters have just gone past."

Oliver and Scott grinned at each other. John Turner, it seemed, had taught them well.

They did not slow down until they had to stop and check the name of the road.

"Chapel Street!" cried Oliver, pointing in triumph. "Now, where's number 25?"

The newspaper office proved to be right next to a busy supermarket, further along the road than Oliver had thought.

"It's taken us just over twenty minutes," he said,

checking his watch with the Post Office clock opposite. "And that's running most of the way."

"Well, I'm not running all the way back," Said Scott flatly, still panting a little. "If any of my mates at the comprehensive could see me flogging myself stupid to get a paper, they'd think I was cracked! We only need the offices to be closed, or someone telling us they haven't got a copy. or something, and — "

"Shut up, Scotty!" interrupted Oliver. "You're beginning to sound like Jason."

But even he could not resist a sigh of relief when the girl at the counter looked at the page which Tina and Rachel had found and nodded her head.

"Last week's edition, is it?" she enquired brightly, checking the date.

Oliver nearly tore the front page of the *Burford Echo* in his haste to get to page three, and as it started to rain, he and Scott read the full report of the robbery at Melton Grange.

MYSTERY OF VALUABLE CHALICE

Mystery surrounds the theft of the Lady Elizabeth gold chalice stolen from the chapel at Melton Grange School last week. Burford Police had expected to recover the chalice when a gold plate, stolen at the same time, was found on school premises. "We were disappointed at not being able to make an early arrest," said Detective Inspector P. Drew, who is in charge of the case. "But our enquiries are still continuing."

"Anything interesting?" whispered Scott, reading over

Oliver's shoulder, following his finger along the printed lines.

> *Detective Inspector Drew confirmed that a 14-year-old pupil at the school had been questioned, but refused to give any further details at present. "This is at the request of Melton Grange," he said. "Obviously, they have their good reputation to consider."*

"Well." said Oliver after a pause, "at least we know why nobody at Melton Grange wants to talk about the missing chalice."

"Sounds as if that boy's in real trouble," pronounced Scott, watching Oliver carefully folding the *Burford Echo*. "Wonder who he is?"

"I don't know..." Oliver pushed open the door of the office, reaching out a hand to check that the rain had stopped. "But I can tell you something, Scotty. He's got red hair, like yours!"

"What?" gasped Scott, already having to run to catch up with Oliver. "You mean, that guy in the library, yesterday..."

"He thought you were the boy the police had questioned about the Lady Elizabeth chalice. The boy he and his gang never expected to see again!"

"The — the boss?" Scott stammered, Oliver's words hitting him like a thunderbolt. "You're saying it was the boss who grabbed me yesterday?"

"Couldn't have been anyone else, could it? Which means only one thing."

"What?"

"This boy, whoever he is, didn't steal the Lady Elizabeth chalice."

Eight

It took Oliver and Scott much longer than they had expected to get back to Melton Grange, because the heavy rain had made the ground wet and muddy.

"I'll be glad to get these socks and joggers off," Scott grumbled, as they tried to find the door to the Great Hall.

"Hey, isn't that Jason!" cried Scott suddenly. "What does he look like, eh? I'm certain that straw hat goes with Suzy's Mother Goose outfit."

Dressed in a baggy shirt and old waistcoat, and with his trousers rolled up above his ankles, Jason was quite the hero in Oliver's eyes, as he led them inside.

"What the heck happened to you? Lynsey's been ranting on for ages, and if you don't – "

"We've got the report on the Lady Elizabeth chalice," said Oliver shortly.

"No kidding?" Jason's mood changed completely, eyes gleaming behind his thick glasses. "Anything about the boss?"

"Well," began Scott, sitting himself down on the edge of the windowsill, "there's this Detective Inspector Drew in charge of the case, and – "

"Save it until later, Scotty," Oliver ordered impatiently, pulling him off his perch. "Right now, we've got to work out some way of getting back into the session without Lynsey asking too many questions."

"How far have you got?" he continued, turning to Jason.

"It's the end of the second crowd scene, an American

square dance party. Tina and Suzy worked it out between them."

"Brilliant!" Oliver perked up almost immediately, peeling off his trainer shoes and his damp socks and clearly enjoying the surprise on Scott's face.

"I'd better get going," said Jason, backing away hurriedly and pushing the door open. Lynsey's voice carried through from the Great Hall: "I'm giving that pair another five minutes to put in an appearance! If they don't show up then, they're going to be in real trouble!"

"They're just in the washroom, Lynsey," Jason called out. "Be ready in a sec!"

"Keep your fingers crossed!" he muttered to Tina and Rachel. "Ollie's cooking up some idea to be in the square dance scene!"

Afterwards, Jason wondered why he hadn't thought of it, himself. All Oliver and Scott did was to copy him and roll up their trousers, with Scott wearing his T—shirt loose, and Oliver undoing his jacket to show his open-necked shirt. His wet, curly hair was combed to make it flatter, than parted in the middle. And at the last minute, Scott added one or two ragged patches torn from paper hand-towels.

Seeing them sauntering back into the Great Hall, Lynsey quite forgot the telling-off she'd had in mind.

"Still can't see why you spent so long getting ready for the part," she commented drily, eyeing their bare feet, "but I suppose the waiting was worth it. John Turner gave us a good report for the pirate scene, and there's no reason why he shouldn't do the same again."

"Just as long as I don't have to do too much dancing," Oliver confided to Tina. "I've got the *Burford Echo* tucked down the back of my joggers."

There was only a half-hour break before the start of the

stage make-up demonstration, so Jason, Tina and Rachel lost no time sneaking into the washroom to read what it said in the *Burford Echo* about the stolen chalice.

"Ollie," said Rachel, "why do you say that this other boy the police questioned has got red hair like Scott? Is it anything to do with the man nabbing Scotty in the library?"

"Yes, because he thought Scotty *was* that boy."

"And those voices we heard coming from our bedroom, talking about the boss," Jason remembered thoughtfully. "We wondered then why anyone was up there. But, if they'd seen Scotty's red hair from outside — "

"They'd think it was this other red-haired boy, too," gasped Rachel. "Same as the man in the library yesterday."

"And I bet the man knows the boy didn't take the Lady Elizabeth chalice!" exclaimed Oliver. "Otherwise, why didn't he tell the police or Fellowes or somebody that he thought he'd seen the thief in the library? Why come out with all those threats about what's going to happen if he stays anywhere near Melton Grange?"

"Trying to scare him off?" suggested Jason, after a pause. "Wanting to make sure the boy keeps out of the way."

"Right! Know why? Because he wants to get his hands on the chalice! Because he's the boss who's got to be tracked down before the drama festival finishes!"

There was quite a long silence as Oliver's words sank in. Then Rachel asked the question which was on all their minds.

"So what about the other red-haired boy, Ollie? Why were the police questioning him in the first place?"

Oliver shrugged his shoulders. "If he knew where the chalice is, that was his chance to tell the police and get himself out of trouble, wasn't it? And if he doesn't know where it is," he paused, taking a deep breath, "I don't see how he could have anything to do with the robbery."

"There was that red-haired person I saw at the window," began Tina timidly, but the others were too busy turning to see what the din was at the back of the Great Hall, Oliver hastily stuffing the *Burford Echo* inside his shirt.

"You lot still here?" cried Mark from the Langham Theatre Group, sounding surprisingly cheerful for somebody weighed down with two stage lamps and trying to kick a heavy box through the swing doors. "Great! We could do with a bit of help, getting Betty's gear fixed up."

"Betty?" echoed Jason blankly. "Oh, you mean Madame Helga!" He and Rachel hurriedly stepped out of the way of a huge mirror being carried on to the stage. "What's all this in aid of?"

"Doing the demonstrations on stage make-up, isn't she?" Mark sounded surprised that Jason needed to ask. "She teaches all the Langham Theatre School students."

"You must be experts, then!" said Scott at once. He meant it to be a crafty dig at Langham, but Amanda answered him quite seriously.

"Guess you could say that. Madame keeps us all up to the mark, anyway."

"Not that we'd ever be as good as the make-up artists she's taught!" added Lynette. "Some of them are the best in the country!"

"Madame Helga?" said Rachel, just to make sure they were talking about the same person.

"Doing the make-up demonstrations?" echoed Tina in disbelief.

"OK, don't keep on about it," snapped Mark, thinking Studio Workshop were getting ready to play some kind of joke. "If you don't feel like lending a hand, just say so."

"Who said we wouldn't help?" demanded Oliver, giving Scott a push. "Come on, Scotty!"

"Where do you want these two big stands for the

dressing table mirrors?" Scott asked, getting ready to lift one. "Up-stage? Stage right? Don't want to get too much shadow from the overhead lights."

There was almost a hush of respect from the Langham group.

"No need to unwind all the wire for the stage lamps and have it trailing all over the place. Let's have the mirrors facing the audience, with the chairs in front, and have an extra one to use as a spare table. And lay all the boxes out in a row."

"None of us have had to be stagehands before," puffed Amanda, helping Jason to set the last mirror in place. "Madame Helga's always got somebody else to do the donkey work."

"We guessed that!" grinned Jason, and Amanda smiled back at him. "Still, you know more than us about make-up, so that evens things up a bit, doesn't it?"

He could tell that Amanda was wondering how to answer that, when Madame Helga came in.

"What a wonderful set, darlings!" she cried, standing back to admire the stage. "So clever to have the models with their backs to the audience, so that people can see their reflections."

"All Studio Workshop's idea," announced Mark, glad that Madame Helga was so pleased. "Specially Scott, their stage manager. He was the boss."

"The — the boss?"

Rachel couldn't quite decide whether Madame Helga's pink cheeks had suddenly paled a little, or if it was nothing more than the light changing as she stepped up on to the stage.

"Well, a good stage manager must know how to give the right orders! Would you like to be one of my models, dear?"

51

"No, thanks," Scott replied quickly, fingering the plaster on his forehead. It began to dawn on him just how useful a strip of plaster might be, and he wondered whether he could keep it on until the end of the festival.

"Oh, of course, a bump on the head, I quite understand. How about the little girl with the red hair instead? And let's have the blonde beside her."

Tina hated being called a "little girl" and Rachel did not care very much for "the blonde", either. But they soon forgot their resentment when Madame Helga got to work.

"Beautiful skin, this girl has," she announced, talking about Rachel. "Can you see how we make her eyes look bigger with pale greasepaint, and smaller with the darker shades? And don't be afraid to mix colours to get the tints you want."

Then Madame Helga turned to Tina, pushing her a little closer to the stage mirror.

"Lovely red hair, isn't it? But a red-haired person always has an unusual colouring, and it's nearly always a mistake to try and alter it. See what you think of some black eye make-up on these pale lashes and eyebrows."

Tina watched her face being transformed with deft, quick strokes of Madame Helga's make-up brushes and pencils, as if she was painting a picture.

"Looking different already, isn't she?" smiled Madame Helga, gratified by the murmurs of surprise from the audience. "Now, let's change the shape of these eye-brows. . . What do you think, dear?"

"Yes. . . " Tina could hardly take her eyes off her own reflection. "And — would I look more different with — with something over my hair?"

"Most certainly," Madame Helga smiled, reaching across for a hand towel. "See for yourself."

Tina's hands trembled as she tied the towel around her

head, tucking every strand of hair underneath. Then she looked at herself again, studying the face which stared right back at her.

"Quite a transformation, isn't it, dear? A red-head in disguise!"

"Yes." Tina looked again at the thick, sooty-black eyebrows, standing out like ugly smudges. "Yes. Now I know who she is."

Nine

"Tina," groaned Rachel, "how much longer are we going to be stuck here?"

Her voice sounded a bit muffled because they were squashed up against each other, inside the boys' wardrobe.

"Ssssh!" Tina cut in impatiently. "Only a few more minutes. . . "

"How come I got talked into this? I should've known something was on your mind, soon as I saw that look on your face at the end of Madame Helga's make-up session."

"Shouldn't be too long, now." Tina squinted through the crack between the wardrobe doors. "I think somebody's coming!"

She squeezed herself back against a rack of track suits and sweatshirts, listening to the sound of a key slowly turning in the lock. Then someone began moving around the room.

"What's all the mystery?" whispered Rachel. "It's only that tea girl, isn't it?"

"Hold on a sec. Listen, the door's opening again. . . "

"Matthew. . . " The name was spoken in a low whisper, so softly that Rachel wondered whether she'd heard it at all.

"Matthew! Come inside, quickly! I think they're all still at lunch, so you should be all right."

"Can always crawl under the bed, can't I?" Even in a whisper, it was impossible not to hear the bitterness in his voice. "Don't forget to put the latch up on the door, either."

Rachel nudged Tina out into the room. "Sorry about this, but I couldn't stand it in that wardrobe a minute longer!"

Seeing the look on Tina's face, she protested: "Well, you said we only had to wait until they came in."

The thick, black eyebrows stood out even more clearly with Kate's face so drawn and pale. She began fingering the scarf around her head, but as she sank down on the edge of Jason's bed, it slid down to reveal a mass of thick, red hair, the same as the boy standing against the wall.

"Don't cry, Kate," begged Tina, seeing she was near to tears. "We won't say anything about your brother being here."

"My — my brother?" Kate covered her face with her hands, shaking her head miserably. "So, you know. . . "

"How did you find out?" asked the boy curtly. "Who's been talking?"

"Nobody." Tina watched Kate dabbing her eyes with a handkerchief. "The black eyebrows and the lashes gave it away, really. That, and the hair. I kept wondering what it was about your face, Kate. Then, at this make-up demonstration, I saw myself in a mirror. It was a bit like looking at you."

"What else do you know?" asked Matthew. His face was grim and unsmiling, and in his blue polo-neck sweater and faded jeans, he seemed much older than Scott. "That I've been held by the police? That I'm supposed to have stolen the Lady Elizabeth chalice? That I'm due to be expelled for something I didn't do?"

Kate had begun weeping again, black watery smudges all around her eyes. This was more than tender-hearted Tina could bear.

"Don't cry," she pleaded, taking Kate's hand. "Please, don't."

"And you can stop feeling sorry for yourself," Rachel burst out, rounding on Matthew so unexpectedly that he shrank back in surprise. "D'you think it helps your sister,

55

or anyone else, hearing your hard luck story?"

"Hey, just you wait a minute," Matthew stepped forward, his brown eyes glaring at her. "If you think this is any picnic — "

"Oh, don't waste time arguing!" cried Tina. "There's only about an hour before we've got to go downstairs for rehearsals."

"Rehearsals!" Matthew gave a hollow laugh. "Hah! You can cast me as the villain, any day of the week. You know? The guy who gets all the boos and the hisses."

Fortunately, he was saved from another lashing by Rachel's tongue by a quiet tap at the door.

"Hi! Can we come in?"

"Oliver!" Tina called with relief, almost flying across the room. "I told him to give us about ten minutes before coming up."

She pushed up the latch and turned the key as carefully as she could, opening the door just wide enough for Oliver, Jason and Scott to creep inside.

It was quite a squash with the seven of them in the little room. Being crammed together, they all felt quite sheepish, and there were a few moments' silence.

Then Matthew looked across at Scott, and Scott looked at Matthew.

"Well," breathed Matthew at last. "No wonder you thought I'd turned up out of the blue when this one arrived, Kate. I bet I'd have dropped the tea-tray, too."

"And that was the first time I heard somebody talking about the boss, Matthew. Remember, I told you?"

"We heard that, as well," Jason cut in. "'Course, we didn't know anything about the missing chalice then, not until Tina found the paper in the drawer."

"The Lady Elizabeth gold chalice!" Matthew groaned, clutching at his red hair. "Look, whatever anyone says, I

56

didn't take it. But, somehow, I've got to find the thing before the Head gets back after half term. That's why I'm still here."

"So, what made the police question you?" asked Oliver. "And what about your mum and your dad? Couldn't they do something?"

"It isn't as easy as that," Matthew sighed again, glancing across at his sister. "Oh, Kate's much better at explaining all this than I am."

In the end, there wasn't much to tell. Their father was an army officer serving abroad. Matthew spent the school holidays with Kate, while she studied at a nearby college.

"And we've got an old aunt who's meant to keep an eye on things," Matthew chipped in.

The Lady Elizabeth chalice, he told them, dated from Tudor times, named after one of the ladies-in-waiting to the great Queen Elizabeth, whose family home had been at Melton Grange. It had been kept under lock and key in the school chapel for many years, and only brought out on special occasions.

"But I decided to do a special project about it. You know, finding out who the owners had been, who made it, when and where it had been used – all that sort of thing. So I was allowed to take photographs and make drawings. Doctor Cole said it would be part of a published history of Melton Grange."

"And that was when it was stolen?" said Jason, making a guess.

"Yes. Everyone else had gone home for half term when it happened, so I was the only one here. Narrowed things down for the police quite nicely, didn't it? I was packing my gear when they found the matching gold plate in my room. That's why they think I stole the chalice."

"He's meant to be staying with Aunt Mary," finished

57

Kate. "Only I knew she was off on holiday with her friend, so I got this temp job helping with the drama festival. The rest you know."

"All the same, Matthew," said Scott, taking a deep breath, "someone knows full well that you didn't pinch the Lady Elizabeth chalice." And he went on to tell him about the incident in the school library. "Ollie reckons that guy could have been the boss, the brains behind all this, the one everyone's been talking about."

"Oh, heck!" Matthew clutched at his hair again. "The same sort of thing happened to me in the Great Hall, just before the police were called in. I told them about it, but they didn't believe me. Who would?"

"And wasn't that when you heard somebody mentioning the boss, too?" prompted Kate.

"Yes, but that was when I'd got back to my room. Sounded a bit like Fellowes, I thought."

"Fellowes?" Jason almost spat out the name. "He's the one who wanted to send Scotty home. A right shady character, if you ask me."

"Oh, I don't know what to believe." Matthew clutched at his hair again. "But if you say the boss is hanging around, it must mean there's a chance the chalice is still here, somewhere. And that's what I thought."

"So, where do you hide out, Matthew?" asked Oliver.

"One of those lobbies on the landing, mostly. It's not too bad."

"Why don't you stay up here, with us? If anyone sees you, they'll probably think it's Scotty. You aren't much taller than him, are you? It'll be easier if we're all together on this."

His digital watch began bleeping loudly.

"Hey, we're meant to be at rehearsals! Look, Matthew, any chance of us seeing this project you were working on?

You said something about photos and drawings and that. It'd give us some idea of what we're meant to be searching for."

"Yes, that's a point." Tina was pleased to see Matthew cheering up, now that he knew he and Kate had friends who believed him and wanted to help.

"I'll get the folder and bring it straight up," offered Kate, hurrying towards the door. "Shan't be a moment."

"We'll come with you," said Oliver, eyes on his watch again. "Otherwise Lynsey will be coming up to see what's keeping us."

"Thanks, Oliver," whispered Matthew, as they all went out. "See you a bit later on."

They began following Kate down the little flight of stairs as quietly as they could, with Scott and Oliver looking over their shoulders to make sure nobody was in sight, listening and watching.

"I wondered what all these doors were for," said Scott, determined to make everything sound completely normal, as if it were quite usual for Studio Workshop to get mixed up with robberies, stolen chalices and unseen gangland bosses.

"Mostly broom cupboards and storage spaces, I'm afraid," smiled Kate, fingering her scarf again. "Now, mind these first three steps. I'm always tripping up, the way they curve round..."

Her words faltered to a stop, staring down at the mass of papers and diagrams scattered all over the tiny staircase, a coloured photograph dangerously near the toe of her shoe.

"Quick, let's get this lot cleared up before anyone sees," hissed Oliver urgently. "All this belongs to Matthew, doesn't it, Kate?"

She nodded her head dumbly, taking the photograph in

both hands, her eyes wide and staring.

"Yes," she said, at last. "Yes, this is one of Matthew's shots of the Lady Elizabeth chalice. He kept it in a special folder — and nobody knew where that was. Only him, and me."

"And now somebody's tried pinching it," said Jason huskily, helping Tina and Rachel to gather up the rest of the papers. "They might have got away with it, too, if we hadn't come out of our room when we did."

"So that means the boss must have had somebody listening at the door," declared Rachel in disgust. "He's watching every single move we make."

Ten

"Oliver!" A shrill voice shouted up from the floor below, making them all jump. "Rachel! Lynsey says rehearsals have started, and when are you coming down?"

"That's Suzy," whispered Rachel, and she called back over the bannisters. "OK, we're coming right this minute."

"Tell Lynsey I've had to go back for something," suggested Oliver in a low voice. "Say I won't be long!"

"Oh, Oliver," Kate sighed, fingering Matthew's photo of the Lady Elizabeth chalice. "We seem to be bringing you nothing but trouble."

"Had to find out why somebody was setting about Scotty, didn't we?" Oliver pointed out reasonably. "Come on, let's see if there's anything else missing from that project folder, while we've got the chance."

Kate unlocked one of the little doors and switched on a light to show the inside of a tiny lobby. It was only a bit bigger than an ordinary broom cupboard, with boxes and cartons of cleaning stuffs lining the shelves on one side.

"Wouldn't think there was enough space for Matt's sleeping bag, would you?" she said shakily, looking around. "He thought he was lucky to have an air vent."

"Now," she continued, feeling along a half-empty shelf, "this is where I keep my cleaning basket, and I put Matthew's folder right at the back, in an old carrier bag. I didn't think anyone else would even think of coming in here, you see."

"Not until somebody heard him telling us where the

61

folder was," said Oliver, taking care to keep his voice down to a whisper. "And without your cleaning basket hiding it, I bet the thief thought it was his lucky day."

"Lucky he didn't see the carrier bag was practically falling to bits," said Kate, trying to smile. "I don't think he got away with much."

"Oliver!" yelled another voice – Daniel, this time. "Oliver, Lynsey says – "

"All right, I'm coming!"

"Be careful, Oliver," Kate called softly. "Whoever it is behind all this, they – well, they must know you're helping Matthew, now. And they've probably guessed who I am, too."

"Don't worry, we'll be back as soon as we can," he promised her, dashing down the stairs before she could answer. "Tell Matthew we'll give two taps on the door, so he'll know it's us."

It was very difficult to concentrate on rehearsals for *The Merrie Devil of Dreyton* with so much on their minds. Oliver could tell that Jason and Scott wanted to know what had happened – but them being late had put Lynsey very much on her guard.

"We're waiting for you, Oliver," she told him, over and over again, until, everyone was tired of hearing it. "Look, are you in this production, or not?"

"Sorry, Lynsey... " There didn't seem much else he could say.

"I just don't know what's got into you, this afternoon. Jason and Scott are almost as bad."

Scott said nothing, but Rachel could see he was squirming inside. She took a deep breath and stepped forward, ready to act her part. "The show must go on!" was one of Lynsey's pet sayings. Now, Rachel thought she was beginning to understand what that really meant.

"Good morrow, Edwin! A job for you to do!
My father's horse has dropped a shoe!"

Seeing the old play being performed again was beginning to put new heart into Oliver and Jason, too. They both remembered how they had finally traced the script, which had been forgotten for nearly two hundred years, copying out the parts by hand at the Castle Museum.

Surely, Oliver told himself, it couldn't be much more difficult to find something like a gold chalice, missing for just over a week and hidden right under their noses?

"But, do we find the boss, and then the chalice?" he wondered. "Or, is it the chalice that leads us to the boss?"

He spoke without thinking, trying to work it all out in his mind, surprised when Jason nodded his head knowingly.

"Just what I was thinking, Ollie! After all, if the boss is still around somewhere, he must be after the chalice, same as we are! And he's got to get it before next week, because that's when the Head comes back, like Matthew said. Obvious, really, isn't it?"

"Brilliant," growled Oliver. "So where's the obvious place for hiding a gold chalice, and finding the boss, tell me that."

Unfortunately, Lynsey happened to catch the last bit of what he said, her green eyes blazing once more.

"I'll tell you something, Oliver Davis! That's the third cue you've missed in the space of ten minutes, so if you can't follow the script – "

"Yes – OK, Lynsey. I'm sorry. . . "

"Right," Lynsey sighed wearily. "Let's take it from the top, where the Squire hears about Edwin and Lord Cuthbert both wanting to marry Mathilda. Come along, Daniel!"

"We'll settle this! Now, all around, attend!
To Dreyton, now, both sweethearts we will send!
And he who dares to sleep all night
In my Whispering Chamber, without fear or fright,
Shall win the girl! Good Cuthbert, don't be taunted!
For, by my ruff, I can't believe 'tis haunted!"

"Any idea how we'll manage the black background for the scene in the haunted chamber, Scott?" asked Lynsey, looking up from the script. "We must keep the effect of Firefly's demons appearing in the dark and scaring Lord Cuthbert."

"No problem," said Scott, suddenly thoughtful, "as long as we can roll our black curtain from the back of the stage. Any chance of us nosing around — er, I mean, going backstage, to see how we could fix it? We'll have to wire up microphones for the spooky sound effects, as well."

"Yes, I'm sure that will be all right," smiled Lynsey, pleased to see Scott's enthusiasm returning. "I'll speak to John Turner as soon as I can, and let you know."

"Great!" Scott was so excited, he even dared to give a "thumbs up" sign to Oliver, just as he was beginning his next speech as John Gabriel, the blacksmith.

"Hey," whispered Jason, seeing the look of understanding which flashed between them, "what's going on, Scotty?"

"Nothing, yet," grinned Scott, folding his arms. "But I reckon we'll soon be getting the go-ahead to start searching for that chalice!"

The rest of the rehearsal went without too many hitches, smoothly enough for Lynsey to smile at the end of the last scene.

"Not too bad, after all, was it? We'll have some more

rehearsal time, tomorrow, so you can all have an evening off in the television and games room."

There was a murmur of approval, followed by the usual buzz of chatter as everyone began collecting their props and folding costumes, ready to leave the rehearsal room. After such a hectic day, it was nice to look forward to a few hours to themselves.

Scott, of course, had other ideas.

"We ought to get back to Matthew, right after supper," he told Oliver, between mouthfuls of cheese-and-potato pie. "Once we've got a few ideas from him about where to start looking for that chalice, we can really get going."

"And what about the rest of us?" demanded Rachel. "It's asking for trouble if we all go off and start nosing around, even with a cast iron excuse about doing work on our production."

"You and Tina go to the games room with the others, then." Oliver suggested. "As long as you two show your faces, nobody will take much notice if we're not there."

Tina would much rather have been going up to the fifth floor with the boys. But she could see that what Oliver and Rachel said made a lot of sense.

"Ask Matthew if he wants us to bring him anything to eat, won't you?" she said — something Oliver hadn't thought of. "We can always get something from the cafeteria."

After that, Rachel and Tina tried not to think about the boys getting the tiny service lift to the fourth floor, walking up the stairs, than making their way along the little landing which they now knew so well.

Instead, they settled comfortably in front of the huge television set, the thought never crossing their minds that this might be exactly where Matthew wished he was, right at that moment.

"Seems ages since I could just sit and watch TV," he was telling Scott and Jason. Oliver was helping him sort through the project folder. "Still, this is ten times better than being caged in downstairs. Any more pages missing, Ollie?"

"No, only those two you spotted, right at the end. And you said there was another copy of the photograph?"

"Yes." He passed the photograph across, so that Jason and Scott could see the Lady Elizabeth gold chalice in every detail – the handles studded with precious stones, the carvings around the bowl and on the base, the soft gleam of the ancient gold inside. "Now you can see why somebody wants to get their hands on it, eh?"

"Anyway," he continued, "I think Scott's right about starting the search in the Great Hall."

"But why the Great Hall?" asked Jason. "Reckon that's where somebody's hidden the chalice?"

"I don't know. But, it's where I was threatened by that thug, wasn't it? The same way that Scott was, when he went back into the library. Those are the only places at Melton Grange where we know for sure the boss has been. And, as the library's mostly closed. . . "

"It's the Great Hall to start with!" agreed Scott. "The question is, where do we kick off? Any clues, Matt? Secret cupboards, hidden cubby-holes, that sort of thing?"

Matthew smiled broadly, getting up from the edge of Jason's bed and stretching himself.

"If there are, it's all been kept so secret that nobody knows about them. But I'll show you something that's nearly as good. Make sure the coast is clear, Oliver, then we'll go down to the lobby."

They crept along the landing and down the stairs, Matthew keeping well back in the shadows. It was even darker inside the lobby, with nobody daring to put on the light, but Scott's sharp eyes picked out a thin wispy glow near the floor.

"Where's that coming from?" he asked Matthew.

"Lift that loose bit of wood away," Matthew whispered back. "Then you'll see."

It was more like a long wooden wedge, Scott thought, but he managed to pull it free much more easily than he expected.

"I — I don't believe it," he muttered. "It — it's the Great Hall. We're looking down on the Great Hall."

"Right behind one of the displays on the walls," confirmed Matthew. "See anything interesting?"

"No, not much. . . " Scott sounded a bit disappointed, but it was enough to make Jason wriggle along the lobby floor beside him.

"What d'you mean, not much? Can't you see who's just coming up to the stage, rabbiting away, there?"

"Madame Helga!"

"And Fellowes!" Jason nodded in the darkness. "Looks like they know each other pretty well, doesn't it?"

"Yes, you are quite right, Helga." Fellowes never spoke loudly, but his voice sounded surprisingly clear in the tiny lobby. "We must keep a sharp look-out for the boss. Most important, I agree."

"Well," breathed Scott, under his breath. "How about that?"

"I said Fellowes was a shady character," whispered Jason. "And I was right!"

Eleven

None of the boys got much sleep that night.

"Old Fellowes, though," Matthew kept whispering, propping himself up on one elbow and staring out at the darkness. "I still can't believe it! Who'd have thought he'd be working for the boss?"

"You heard what he said to Madame Helga," Scott reminded him drowsily.

"Yes, but in the Great Hall?" Matthew whispered back. "Surely they could have found somewhere a bit more private."

"Didn't know we'd be listening, did they?" mumbled Oliver, determined to keep his eyes firmly shut. "Look, Matt, go to sleep, can't you? It's been a long day."

"Sorry." Matthew snuggled down into his sleeping bag again. So many thoughts flitted through his mind. Where was the missing chalice? Who had stolen it? How had the gold plate got into his room? And who was the mysterious boss Madame Helga and Fellowes were working for?

But the prospect of being expelled for the theft seemed so much like a strange, terrible nightmare, that he at last fell into a troubled sleep, glad to wake up and hear the rain pattering on the window.

"Looks like it's worse than yesterday," commented Jason, putting on his glasses to peer out at black skies. "Might get a chance to start working on the sound effects Scotty."

"Hope so! We know Lynsey's got rehearsals lined up this morning, but there's nothing to stop us making a start later on."

"I was just thinking," he went on, helping Matthew to roll up his sleeping bag. "Couldn't we use that spy-hole in the lobby for some of the sound effects? The audience would never guess where all the moans and groans were coming from."

"I can just imagine," grinned Matthew. "You wouldn't think all those little lobbies around the stairs were once part of a loft above the Great Hall, would you? That was until the ceiling was raised and this floor added for the servants' quarters – oh, well over a hundred years ago."

"So, in those days, we'd have been looking out into the main loft, instead of the Great Hall?" mused Oliver. "I get it. . . "

"And that's where the little door would have been," added Matthew, proceeding to stuff the sleeping bag in the bottom of the wardrobe. "Then once the door was walled, a doorway was fitted at the other end, leading off the staircase going up to this floor."

"You seem to know a terrific lot about Melton Grange," observed Oliver, once all the details had sunk in.

"It's more or less what I found out through doing the work on the Lady Elizabeth chalice. It was always used for special prayers, whenever a servant got married, or if anyone left the household. . . "

His voice trailed away, seeing Oliver putting a finger to his lips.

"Who is it?"

"Mickey Mouse!" came the answer. "Hurry up, Oliver, let us in."

"We'll have to think of a special knock or something, so you'll know it's us," complained Rachel, flouncing into the room. She always hated being kept waiting. "We were all set to call in again last night. But the light was out, and we didn't want to give you a scare."

"You must've been late getting up," said Oliver quickly. "How come?"

"What d'you think?" Tina broke in. "Madame Helga and that man Fellowes were talking together for ages. Rachel thought something was funny when he nipped into the TV room, then went out again – you know, as if he was looking for somebody."

"Did he say anything?" Jason interrupted.

"No. And then Mark and Amanda and a few others from Langham Theatre came in, and Mark said something like: 'Where's our Betty, this evening?' That started us thinking."

"They ended up in the Great Hall," said Rachel, taking up the story with relish. "Couldn't hear what they were taking about, but – Hey, why are you looking at each other like that? What's been going on that we don't know about?"

"Not much, Ratchet," grinned Jason, with another glance at Oliver. "Ollie will tell you."

Matthew leaned back against the wall, trying to decide once again whether or not he could believe what Oliver was saying. Rachel seemed just as bewildered as he was.

"Fellowes? Working for the boss? But, how? I mean, what's he supposed to be doing?"

"Trying to find where the chalice has been hidden," contributed Jason with an air of triumph. "Then he passes on the info to Mr Big."

"I still don't understand," said Rachel flatly. "Someone comes to Melton Grange, pinches the chalice, hides it somewhere for the boss to collect – yet nobody knows where it is?"

"But if Fellowes and Madame Helga were talking about the boss, they must know something," Scott pointed out. "We've got to keep an eye on those two."

"Yes..." Jason nodded slowly. "But that might not get us anywhere before the end of the festival. The thing is to get them both talking... without them knowing exactly what we're after..."

Matthew glanced questioningly at Oliver, but he simply shrugged his shoulders with a look of long-suffering patience. They all knew that Jason took a lot of understanding at times!

"Watch it," grinned Scott, seeing him frowning hard and chewing one end of his glasses. "Jason's brain is starting to work overtime."

He was right. All through breakfast, Jason hardly spoke, biting off a piece of toast, then tearing the slice into tiny pieces, staring at the sugar bowl. He drank nearly all Rachel's grapefruit juice before it dawned on him that it wasn't a bit like his usual orange, and then wondered why the cornflakes tasted warm and soggy.

"Jason!" bellowed Oliver, so loudly that everyone turned round to see what was going on. "Tina's just said,. that's the coffee pot, not the milk jug. Didn't you hear?"

"No! Really?" Jason gazed at the coffee pot as if he had never seen one before, then took another mouthful of murky brown cornflakes.

They were glad to see Kate coming over with the trolley. Hearing Oliver yelling at Jason had given her a good excuse to speak to them. "Plenty more coffee here!"

"I'll take this half empty one up to Matthew," she whispered, bending over the table to exchange coffee pots. "He does love a cup of coffee."

"Kate," Jason broke in, tugging gently at her overall. "Kate, listen! That photograph of the Lady Elizabeth chalice. You know, the one we found on the stairs yesterday?" Kate nodded. "Has Matthew got more than one copy? I mean, could we borrow the one he's got? And maybe a few more as well?"

"Well," Kate hesitated, wondering what was coming

next, "I can always get some extra copies printed, Jason. And if it's to help Matthew..."

"Oh, yes!" he cried, suddenly looking very pleased . "It's to help him, all right! Reckon you and Matthew can sort something out by lunchtime?"

"I — I'll try Jason..." It was clear that Kate wanted to ask a few more questions but just at that moment Lynsey called across from Sara and Daniel's table.

"I hope you aren't going to sit there gossiping all morning, you lot. Rehearsals start at ten o'clock sharp, and I don't want you turning up late again."

"Just finishing the coffee, Lynsey," Scott grinned back, holding up his steaming cup to prove it. "What did John Turner say about us fixing the sound effects?"

"Basically, you can go ahead. Just as long as you don't make a nuisance of yourself."

"Scotty?" laughed Oliver. "He never stops being a nuisance."

"She was talking about all of us," Scott retorted, giving Oliver a push. "Why didn't you stick up for me, Jason?"

"Jason," hissed Tina, and grabbed his shoulder. "Jason, did you hear what Scott said?"

"Eh?" The thick glasses were taken off, then put back on again. "Yes, that's great, Scott. We can get on with the sound effects."

Rachel and Tina shook their heads at each other, slow smiles spreading across their faces.

"Come on, Jason!" said Rachel kindly, taking him by the arm. "Time to get back to earth!"

They half expected him to do a lousy rehearsal and put Lynsey in a bad mood again. But he didn't. Instead, he seemed to be concentrating harder than any of them.

"And it will be wrong, if Matthew gets expelled for something he didn't do," said Jason in a low voice, when both he and Oliver were off stage. "Melton Grange won't ever get the Lady Elizabeth chalice back, either, unless we try and help."

"I know," Oliver agreed with a deep-felt sigh. "But where do we go from here? And while I think of it – why did you want those photos of the Lady Elizabeth chalice, all of a sudden?"

"Eh?" Jason looked around vaguely, then glanced at his watch, dropping his script in the process. "Oh, thanks for reminding me, Ollie. D'you reckon Rachel will get through her part early?"

"Rachel?" echoed Oliver. "What's Rachel got to do with it?"

Jason smiled, his face clearing suddenly, making him look very much down-to-earth.

"Rachel? I thought she'd be best, coming with me and Lynsey. When we go to show the photos of the Lady Elizabeth chalice to Fellowes."

Twelve

Lynsey always had a break half-way through rehearsals, so Rachel and Jason were able to go back upstairs and see the photographs Matthew had sorted out.

"Take whatever you want," he said, waving a hand towards the collection spread out on Oliver's bed. "Kate's got the negatives for all these, so it doesn't matter about getting them back."

"Brilliant!" declared Jason, picking out two of the colour prints. "Are there any here that nobody's seen, Matthew?"

Matthew shook his head.

"Shouldn't think anyone's seen them. Not unless you count the police, and the boss, or whoever it was who tried stealing my folder. And he couldn't have had much chance to get a good look."

"Come on, Jason," said Rachel, tapping her foot impatiently.

"OK, OK," Jason grabbed a few more photos, jerking back in surprise when Kate clutched at his arm.

"Jason, please... you will be careful, won't you? Once the boss hears about this, he's bound to get more desperate – specially if he thinks you're trying to stop him finding that chalice."

"Why d'you think we're getting Lynsey to come with us? She'll know how to handle Fellowes when he starts ranting and raving, wanting to know how we've found him out." He stuffed the photographs in the wallet belonging to Scott's cassette recorder and turned round. "You ready, Ratchet?"

Matthew was amused to hear Rachel huffing out a deep

you heard, dear?" she added in hushed tones. "The police found a gold plate in his study, but they can't find where he's hidden the chalice, Fellowes says. Probably put it in hiding somewhere, ready to collect when all the fuss has died down. That's what they usually do, isn't it? After all, there are plenty of collectors ready to pay thousands for something like that."

"Do you know any collectors, then?" asked Rachel, most politely. The question seemed to annoy Madame Helga, and she glared angrily over her shoulder.

"I was speaking to Miss Ronald," she snapped.

"Rachel and Jason happened to be with me when I found the photographs," Lynsey explained hastily, anxious to avoid any more upsets. "You remember Rachel from yesterday's make-up session, don't you?"

Madame Helga gave a snort which could have meant anything, then tapped gently on a brown, polished door, marked "JANITOR".

"Reginald!" she called, so sweetly that Jason and Rachel could not resist grinning at each other. "Reginald, can you spare a moment?"

After the way Madame Helga had ignored them, Rachel and Jason were quite surprised to find Fellowes ushering them into his office without any arguments.

"I'm so sorry, Reginald," Madame Helga was saying, "but these photographs have just been found. And, of course, I had to explain why they were so important."

"Yes. Yes, of course. Foolish, perhaps, to imagine that we could keep such an affair private, but I did hope the good name of Melton Grange could be protected, at least until the Headmaster returns."

This was not at all what Jason and Rachel were prepared for. They had been expecting to catch Fellowes off guard, to make him blurt out something which would have given them a lead, at least some clue to work on. Seeing him staring at the pictures, suddenly appearing tired and shaken, was completely opposite to what Jason had imagined would happen.

"The boss!" he burst out in desperation. "What about the boss?"

Fellowes looked up sharply, a hint of pride coming back in the way he squared his shoulders and lifted his chin. Had he been bluffing them all along, Jason wondered again?

"The boss?" None of them could mistake the amazement in his reply. "Which boss are you talking about? What on earth has a boss got to do with all this?"

"I think the young man means the person in charge of the investigation, Reginald!" Madame Helga smiled patiently. "Studio Workshop aren't the art experts, you know."

"Ah, yes, of course. Inspector Drew, Burford Police Station. Yes, I shall certainly let him know about these photographs."

Fellowes got up from behind his desk and went over to the door.

"Now, if you will excuse me, I must attend to my other duties."

"Well!" exclaimed Lynsey as they all squeezed into the service lift. "You'd have thought he'd be pleased, or grateful, or interested, or something. Instead, he looked so pathetic, so miserable."

"And sad," sighed Rachel. "So, unless he's a really good actor – "

"Nobody is that good an actor," Lynsey broke in gently, pulling back the lift doors at the fourth floor. "Absolutely nobody."

Jason was too disappointed to say much. He had planned everything so carefully. But they were no further forward than when they started. What could they say to Matthew?

He noticed that the door to the boys' room was half open.

"It's me," he called softly, giving the usual two knocks, "Jason."

He crept into the room, Rachel hovering at the door and looking anxiously inside. Something was wrong, she could feel it — even before she saw that Jason's bed had been pulled out, and the bedclothes thrown around all over the place.

"What's been going on here?" she whispered. "What is it they've been searching for?"

"The boss is behind all this," Jason announced grimly having another look round at the chaos. "He must be!"

"But, what's happened to Ollie and Scott and Tina?" cried
Rachel, almost in tears. "And where's Matthew?"

"Matthew!" Jason cried out, past caring if anyone heard him, or not. "Matthew!"

Rachel held her breath, listening hard.

"What's that, Jason?" she whispered at last. "Can you hear?"

Together they stood in the centre of the room, looking this way and that. And then they heard a voice, faint but not far away.

"Jason! Jason and Rachel, is that you? I'm here! Help me, can't you? Please, help me!"

Thirteen

Rachel and Jason listened hard. Then they heard Matthew's voice again.

"Help! Hey, is anyone there? Help!"

It sounded a bit strange, as if he was some distance away, and yet near — almost like being in a phone box, Jason thought.

"Know something, Ratchet?" he said suddenly. "This is exactly what happened to me and Scotty, the first night at Melton Grange. Remember, when we said we'd heard someone talking about the boss?"

Rachel was busy searching through the wardrobe, pulling out drawers, then peering under all the beds.

"I'm pretty sure nobody else has been in here," she announced. "Nothing's been taken, or even touched. Ollie's bed was a bit untidy, but only because somebody moved it away from the wall — Kate, probably."

"Hey!" They heard Matthew cry out again, sounding closer. "Hey, you two, stop gassing, can't you?"

"Where are you?" Jason called back. looking all round. "Matthew, can you hear me?"

"Jason!" came the reply, followed by two dull thuds. They were not loud, but Rachel felt the floor shake.

"It's coming from underneath the floor. Listen again!"

They got down on their hands and knees, crawling around until they found where the thuds were loudest.

"Over here, by the window, Ratchet. And there's a floorboard that looks a bit loose, as well. Look, right behind Ollie's bed."

The floorboard reminded Rachel of a thick, heavy wedge of cheese as she and Jason struggled to lift it between them.

"Whew!" came Matthew's voice, much nearer this time, and a lot more cheerful. "I thought you'd never get here!"

Jason knelt down at once, poking his head into the hole. He could just make out some wooden struts, made to support the floor of their room, rising up like the rungs of a ladder.

"Where are you, Matt? D'you need any help?"

"Not now I can see where I am!" Matthew's red hair appeared so suddenly through the hole that Rachel jerked back with a little squeal. Threads of soot and dust streaked his face, making his eyes appear bright and staring, his teeth seeming bared in a mad grin.

"Sorry, Rachel! I went to get something from the lobby, and somebody came and slammed the door shut. I thought I'd be stuck there for hours, until I found a sort of hatch which led me along through the old rafters."

With a bit of help from Jason, he managed to haul himself into the room, brushing little showers of dirt from his clothes.

"Sorry," he said again. "I think Kate went looking for you lot, that's after she found she couldn't lift the floorboard by herself."

"So that's why we found the door open," breathed Rachel. "How did you know you could get through to the boys' room, Matthew?"

"Well, once I discovered the hatch, I started working things out. If those lobbies once went all around the old loft, it seemed to me that sooner or later I'd reach this room. I knew it was in the corner of the building, and that made things easier."

There were two taps at the door, and Jason rushed to open it.

"You aren't all that dirty, Matthew," observed Rachel, brushing the last of the soot away. "I'd have thought you'd be covered in dust."

Kate had clearly been thinking along the same lines as Rachel, because she was bustling in with an armful of towels, some soap and a sponge.

"The others are on their way upstairs," she puffed. "I had to rush them out of the dining hall, poor things. How are you feeling, Matt?"

"Fine," he grinned at her. "I knew I'd get out in the end, but it was a bit hairy while I was down there. Boy, was I glad to hear these two."

The story had to be told again when Oliver and Tina and Scott came in, wanting to know what had happened. Scott demanded to see exactly where Matthew had been, then and there, but Oliver wouldn't let him.

"Wait until we've got a few torches, then we can have a really good look," he told Scott. "We want to see exactly where those members of the gang went after they left this room."

"What was it we heard them saying, Scotty?" Jason broke in quietly. "Can you remember, exactly?"

"I reckon so. They said: 'Where is the boss? We've got to get to the boss. Our only chance is to get the boss while this drama festival is going on.' That's about all."

"What made you ask, Jason?" questioned Oliver. "Was it something that Fellowes said, when you showed him Matt's photos of the Lady Elizabeth chalice?"

"Huh!" snorted Rachel before Jason could answer. "Fellowes? He didn't seem to know what day it was. Not even when Jason came right out with it, and asked about the boss."

"*Jason!*" gasped Tina, in a mixture of horror and admiration. "I wouldn't have had the nerve."

"Didn't do much good, though," said Jason dolefully. "All he said was: 'The boss? What on earth has a boss got to do with all this?' Madame Helga was there, with us."

"And did she say anything about the boss?" Scott persisted.

"No, she didn't," Rachel interrupted again. "Only, after Fellowes asked us what the boss had to with the Lady Elizabeth chalice, she came out with a peculiar remark, didn't she, Jason?"

"Yes. She said," he screwed up his eyes, trying to get it right, "she said, 'I think that means the person in charge of the investigation. Studio Workshop aren't the art experts. . .' Something like that, anyway."

There was complete silence in the little room, everyone thinking hard.

"What has a boss got to do with all this. . . " repeated Matthew at last, with a frown, "Doesn't really sound as if he was talking about someone in charge of a gang of crooks, does it?"

"What else could he have meant, then?" Scott retorted impatiently. "I bet that was just a cover-up, because he knew Jason and Rachel were after him."

"And if you think what Madame Helga said, about none of us being art experts," put in Tina, "well, she could have been talking about the Lady Elizabeth chalice, couldn't she?"

There was another pause, then Oliver spoke again, staring down at the floor.

"Whoever Jason and Scotty heard in this room," he said, "they're the ones to go after. Specially now that Matt's found out how they did their disappearing act."

"So, what do we do next, Ollie?" asked Jason, after another pause. "Search round the old lobbies, like Scotty said?"

"We've got some torches in the box of stage gear," supplied Scott helpfully, hauling out the carton patched with sticky-brown paper.

He brandished one torch to demonstrate, but the result was a feeble glimmer of light which flickered bravely, then went out.

"I'll check them for you, Scotty," offered Matthew, pulling the carton towards him and flipping his hand through the cassette spools, the coils of wire and all the other bits and pieces. "It'll give me something useful to do."

Matthew hardly ever complained, Tina reflected on their way to the afternoon session. Sometimes, she tried to imagine how she would feel, being on her own, having to stay in one room and not really knowing much of what was going on. And she knew she wouldn't like it one bit.

"Any sign of Madame Helga?" Jason wondered, breaking into her thoughts as they came into the Great Hall. The Langham Theatre School were already there, grabbing whole batches of seats in the front two rows.

"Hi there, Tina!" Mark was the one who always seemed pleased to see her. "Want to sit with us? Picton Youth Drama are talking about puppet theatre, so you'll want a good view."

"No Madame Helga?" Jason asked innocently, making sure he stayed close behind Tina. "We met up with her after this morning's rehearsals, did she tell you?"

"Was that anything to with the chalice thing she was rambling about, all through lunch?" queried Amanda, after some thought. "She's always going on about antiques, works of art and all that stuff."

"Gets a bit boring, after a while," put in Lynette.

"Even before we got here, she was lecturing us about the wonderful collection of weapons and spears and swords and things at Melton Grange! And we thought we were coming here for a drama festival."

The session proved so popular that "question time" went on for much longer than usual, and the evening meal was late being served.

"Never thought we'd make it!" growled Oliver, clanging the lift doors shut. "Kate has had to go home by now, that's for sure."

"Just as long as Matthew hasn't got fed up waiting and gone with her," joked Scott, but the others were too wound-up to manage a single smile.

Even the lift seemed to take twice as long as usual, so by the time they reached the boys' room, Matthew had already pulled out Oliver's bed and lifted up the floor-board.

"Heavier than it looks, that thing," he commented grimly, sucking at a splinter in his thumb. "Still, I've checked all the torches, and there's more than enough to go round."

There was a sudden feeling of excitement as the torches were passed around and they stood either side of the gap in the floor, watching Matthew lowering himself into the space below.

One by one, they slid down as carefully as they could, feeling for the floor with their feet. Tina was the only one whose legs wouldn't reach, so she jumped, light on her feet as a cat.

"What shall we do about the floorboard?" asked Matthew, shining his torch up through the gap.

"Leave it, until we've found our way around," said Oliver wisely. Ahead he could already see the tiny, hatch-like door, like the one which Matthew had told them about, leading into one of the lobbies. Was this where the gang had made their escape, after Scott and Jason heard them talking about the boss?

"That's the corner of the building," whispered Matthew, flashing his torch to show the rafters again. "We must be right over the stage in the Great Hall."

"And another of those hatches," hissed Scott, ducking under some more rafters. "Wonder where that leads?"

They began creeping forward again, their torches seeming less and less bright the further on they went. Once or twice Scott glanced back over his shoulder, but everything seemed just as it was. Only perhaps darker and more shadowy.

"Funny..." said Matthew, at last. "I'm pretty sure it wasn't as bad as this earlier on. I know it's dark outside, but even so..."

They all heard it at exactly the same moment, a grating sound, like something being dragged across the floor, followed by a slow shudder and a resounding bang.

"Torches off," whispered Oliver. "That was our floor-board being put back."

Fourteen

"Quick," hissed Scott, fumbling in the dark for the handle of the little hatch door. "Go through into the next lobby. Hurry up!"

There was another thud, then a strange sort of dragging noise.

"That's the end of the floorboard being wedged in place," Oliver whispered. "Somebody must be in our room."

"But, who is it?" asked Jason, as loudly as he dared. "Only Fellowes has a key."

"Never mind that now," Matthew rapped out sharply, almost hauling him through the small door. "Get under cover, quick, before you give us all away."

There was the heavy tread of footsteps above them, getting louder as whoever it was began moving along. Then a pause, followed by a bump and a groan of pain.

"You great idiot!" a well-spoken man growled. "Suppose somebody heard that?"

"Do you think I meant to do it?" someone else protested, with another groan. "Oooh, my flaming head. Waste of time trying to get round here without waiting for Shorty, if you ask me."

"Well, nobody is asking you! And I've already explained, we've got to get our hands on that chalice while the Head's out of the way."

"Yes, but it's only Shorty who knows where the boss is."

"He's had to go abroad to do a job for somebody else, hasn't he? How do you think he can get back into Melton Grange once the Head returns?"

Oliver drew in his breath, reaching out a hand to open the hatch door just a little. It was becoming a very interesting conversation.

"Listen, guv, Shorty did it all just the way you wanted. He's the one what pinched the gold plate as well as the chalice, and planted it in that kid's room. Got the cops off our backs very nicely, that did. And when he said the boss with the red tie, I thought you'd know – "

"Well, I didn't. And I'm warning you, if I find those kids from Studio Workshop have been down here – "

"Look, I just put the floorboard back, didn't I? It must've been old Fellowes poking around. How would them kids find a loose floorboard, of all things, when they couldn't even know it was even there."

Matthew was trembling with rage, so angry he could have yelled out loud. In a fit of anger, he stepped forward quickly – too quickly, because he nearly over-balanced after standing in one position for so long, and the ancient woodwork gave a loud creak of protest.

"What was that, guv?" the voice cut through the darkness again, all the wood and the spaces between the lobbies making it muffled, yet just distinct enough for them to hear.

They stood huddled tightly together, watching the yellow beam of a torch wavering behind the hatch door, making some of the old rafters loom in front of them, dark and shadowy. Then the light went off and it was as dark as ever.

"They must be going the other way," breathed Oliver thankfully. "Whew! If those guys had opened that door and shone their torch across the rafters – "

"Don't, Oliver!" begged Tina, shivering once or twice. "Please, don't."

"The question is, how do we get out of here?" demanded Matthew.

"I think the door's locked, or stuck or something," announced Jason, rattling the handle for good measure. "We might have known!"

"Get up off the floor, Scotty!" snapped Rachel. But he beckoned her down.

He slid back a piece of wood in the skirting board, so that Rachel could kneel down and peer into the enormous hall, her eyes on the stage at the far end.

It looked very small, she thought, compared with the displays of swords and shields along the walls. Now that she was closer to them, she could see how huge they were, little golden showers of dust rising up from the warmth of the building.

"Not bad, eh?" said Scott, pleased that Rachel looked so impressed. "Hey, look who's coming in through the corridor, right underneath us. Mabel! Hi, Mabel! Ssssst! Up here!"

For one heart-stopping moment, it seemed she would go without hearing them, her woolly hat pulled down over her ears so that it almost touched the collar of her coat. Then Scott called again, a bit louder this time.

"Mabel! Mabel, up here!"

"Good grief!" She very nearly staggered back, gripping the handle of her shopping basket with both hands. "How on earth did you get up there, Scott?"

"Er, we were working out some sound effects," he told her, "and we sort of lost our way! Be a sport and let us out, Mabel!"

"But, where are you?"

"In one of the lobbies. The one with all the trays and big

dishes and things!"

"Sounds like the Green Suite storeroom to me. Hold on, and I'll see what I can do!"

"How's that for a bit of luck?" grinned Scott. "We'll be back in our room in no time."

"And what about Matt?" demanded Jason. "He can't just walk out of here like the rest of us."

"That's easy. One of can pretend we've lost something so we can go back and let him out. Mabel won't be any the wiser."

"Sounds OK to me," beamed Matthew, and pulled up the collar of his sweatshirt. "Let's hope anyone seeing me thinks it's Scotty going upstairs for an early night."

They all held their breath waiting to hear Mabel's shuffling footsteps outside the storeroom. But once she had managed to push the door open, she barely glanced inside, obviously in a hurry to get home.

"Always been a bother, that door," she confided, already puffing her way back down the stairs. "You'll be all right, now, won't you, dear?"

"Thanks, Mabel," Scott called over the bannisters. "See you tomorrow."

It felt very strange going back into their room. Everything was exactly as they had left it. Nothing had been touched, apart from the floorboard having been wedged back in. There was only Oliver's bed pulled away from the wall to show that anything had happened at all.

"First thing we'll do," he decided, "is put something heavy over this. Then if anyone wants to lift that floorboard again, they're going to be in for a surprise."

"Wonder if this is the way those two crooks got down to the lobbies?" said Jason, helping Scott to haul the box of stage equipment across the floor. "Seems to me they could have gone through one of the hatch doors, maybe,

90

and then seen that the floorboard had been pulled away."

"That's an idea," said Oliver, after some thought. "Then nobody would have needed to come into this room, would they?"

They went on talking far into the night, until Tina leaned against Rachel and closed her eyes. So many questions whirled around inside her head. Who was the man who had ordered Shorty to steal the chalice and put the blame on Matthew? Where could he have hidden it? And what about "the boss with the red tie"?

"Sounds like the boss always wears a red tie, so the crooks know who he is," said Scott.

"So how come it's only Shorty who knows where the boss is?" challenged Oliver. "He's the one who actually pinched the chalice, isn't he?"

"Yes. . ." Jason's deep-sounding voice broke in. "So he must have given it to his boss with the red tie, whoever he is. And now, those two men we heard talking tonight, they've got to track down Shorty's boss so they can collect the chalice from him."

"And they've got to do it while the drama festival's still on," ended Matthew, his red hair seeming to blaze with excitement. "Before the Head comes back and starts asking awkward questions about strangers being at Melton Grange."

"So, why were those two men going through the lobbies in the first place?" asked Rachel, trying not to yawn. "D'you think they were expecting to find a message from the boss, or something?"

"That could be the reason why they didn't want us nosing around down there, Ratchet." Oliver nodded eagerly, rubbing his hands together. "If we could only get our hands on that message from the boss with the red tie, we'd find the chalice, as well."

The boys went on whispering about it long after Rachel and Tina had departed to their own room and everyone else was asleep.

"The boss must have left some clue about the chalice somewhere among the lobbies," Oliver insisted, more than once. "That's why those two men were down there, just like Rachel said."

"Let's start going round all the lobbies as soon as we can, then," Jason suggested. "First thing tomorrow."

"Great!" murmured Matthew, closing his eyes with a warm feeling of hope, deep inside.

He turned over in his sleeping bag, wondering about the two men they had heard. Tina had remarked that they seemed to know their way around Melton Grange. He wished now that he had paid more attention to their voices.

He would talk it over with Kate when she came up to clean the room in the morning. Maybe she could help search some of the lobbies with them, keep a look out for the boss with the red tie — whoever he was. Right now, he was too tired to think about it any longer.

He gave the pillow Jason had lent him one or two thumps, sank his head into the warm hollow, and went to sleep.

He woke in the morning to the sound of brakes squealing and doors being slammed.

"What's going on, Matt?" asked Oliver, blinking hard. "Sounds like a real panic."

"I don't know, Ollie," he faltered, dodging back behind the curtains, "There's at least one police car down there. You — you don't think they've come about the Lady Elizabeth chalice again, do you?"

"Calm down," said Oliver, making an effort to sound calm, himself. "Look, the police have got to keep in contact with Melton Grange over this business, haven't they? You never know, maybe they've got a few leads on the crooks behind it all."

"Yes, but what about all those other people? There must be half a dozen cars parked outside – "

"Quiet, you two," Jason whispered across the room.

There was a clicking of heels on the wooden floor, and a series of brisk-sounding knocks on the door.

"Scott!" called Lynsey sharply. "Are you up, yet?"

"I'm up," Scott called back, "but I'm not dressed."

"Well, come down to the front office as soon as you're ready. And you'd better bring Oliver and Jason as well."

Scott opened the door a chink, and poked his head through.

"Why? Nothing wrong, is there?"

"The police are here and they want to ask you some questions, that's all. Something very serious happened at Melton Grange last night, and it seems you might be able to help them."

Fifteen

The first thing the boys saw when they came downstairs was a blackboard propped against the front desk.

NO ADMITTANCE TO THE GREAT HALL.
SESSIONS FOR THE DRAMA FESTIVAL
WILL RESUME AS SOON AS POSSIBLE.

"See that?" said Oliver, giving Scott a sharp nudge. "Wonder what's been going on?"

There seemed to be a lot of noise, too, with everyone either rushing around or standing in little groups, talking and nodding and pointing in every direction.

In the middle of all the commotion, they almost collided with Tony from Picton Youth Drama and Oliver grabbed at his sleeve.

"Hey, why the panic? What's happened?"

"Haven't you heard? One of those sword displays fell down from the wall last night, crashed straight to the floor! Don't know what the damage is, but there's a rumour going round that it could have been burglars."

None of them knew what to think. They could see Lynsey was trying to smile, coming towards them and putting her arm around Scott.

"Now, I'm sure all this is nothing to worry about, Scott. The police just want to ask you a few questions."

She tapped smartly on the office door and turned the handle. It was quite a surprise to see that John Turner and

Doctor Cole were already there, with Fellowes sitting at his desk, as grim-faced as ever.

The policemen sitting in the chair beside him looked far more friendly, Jason decided. He even got up to shake hands as Lynsey ushered them inside.

"This is Scott, the boy you wanted to see, Inspector Drew. And his friends, Oliver and Jason."

"Please stay if you wish, Miss Ronald," said the inspector. "This is only a matter of routine enquiry." The boys wondered what was coming next.

"Now," he went on, "you probably know that one of the displays in the Great Hall has been dislodged, and we are trying to find out whether that was deliberate, or not. That is where you boys come in." He paused. "I understand you were there last night. Is that correct?"

"Not in the Great Hall, sir," said Scott truthfully. "None of us were."

"Are you sure about that, Scott?" asked John Turner. "I thought I heard you calling to Mabel just as she was going home. Quite late, that was."

"Yes, it was Scott you heard," said Oliver hurriedly. "But we weren't in the Great Hall!"

"We — we got into one of the lobbies on the stairs by mistake," added Scott, carrying on with the story. "And we thought we were locked in. But Mabel gave the door a push and it was OK."

"What were you doing in the lobbies, Scott?" Lynsey broke in. "Working out some of your super sound effects, as usual?"

Before Scott or anyone else could answer, Fellowes suddenly banged on his desk, glaring from one face to another.

"Working out sound effects, indeed! Fooling around! Going into places where you've no business to be!"

"Oh, come now, Fellowes," Doctor Cole broke in soothingly. "These lads weren't to know, were they? Besides, what's kept in those lobbies? Only old bits of equipment, cleaning stuffs and things like that. Nothing worth worrying about."

"So how was it you spoke to Mabel in the Great Hall, Scott?" John Turner persisted.

Scott took a deep breath. "There's a bit in the skirting board that you can slide back. It's just big enough to look through, into the Great Hall – if you lay down flat, that it."

Oliver saw that John Turner and Doctor Cole were grinning at each other, and he began feeling more hopeful.

As long as somebody was on their side, he told himself, they still had a chance. Maybe they wouldn't have to say anything about the loose floorboard in their room and then Matthew would be safe for a bit longer.

"If there was a ten pence piece behind a loose brick halfway up a chimney, that boy would find it," Lynsey was saying, smiling across the room. Only Fellowes continued to sit there, stony-faced.

"So, where was this lobby, Scott?" asked the inspector. "Can you remember?"

"Yes, sir." Scott pondered for a moment. "Mabel said it was the Green Suite storeroom."

"The Green Suite?" echoed Doctor Cole triumphantly, with a sly nod at Fellowes. "That place hasn't been in existence since it was converted into the lower school music room, three years ago. Goodness only knows what junk there must be in the storeroom."

Scott began to feel like the Pied Piper, leading the way up the stairs with Oliver, Jason, Inspector Drew and everyone else following on behind.

"This is the place, sir," announced Scott, pushing open the little door. With so many people trying to squeeze in among the general clutter, there was only just enough room for him to kneel down and point out the piece of wood.

"See," he said, pulling it to one side with a clatter, "this is where I called out to Mabel. There's a proper handle, and everything."

John Turner, Doctor Cole and Inspector Drew all crowded around Scott, eager to see the view into the Great Hall below.

"Oh, of course," breathed Doctor Cole, looking along first in one direction, then the other. "This must have been the school loft, before the floor was removed to make the ceiling of the Great Hall that much higher."

"Miles away from the display that came down, though," observed the police inspector. "You can't even see it from this angle."

"No, this is the end that's nearest the cloakroom," confirmed John Turner. "Roughly where I saw you at yesterday's rehearsals, wasn't it, Scott? Remember? You were working on your sound effects."

"So you didn't see anyone hanging around the Great Hall last night?" insisted Inspector Drew. "Nobody at all?"

"Not after Mabel went home," said Scott. "And that's when we went up to our room."

"I see." The inspector straighted himself up and brushed both sleeves of his uniform with vigour. "So that would have been at least an hour before you locked the Great Hall at eleven o'clock, Mr Fellowes? And you say you saw nothing suspicious?"

"No, indeed, Inspector. I have already told you."

"And it was getting light when I was awoken by this great bang, which must have been the display falling to the floor." Doctor Cole chipped in. "The thing must have fallen down by itself, a wooden peg or a bolt getting weaker over the years, just as I said in the first place! The whole lot needs checking over."

"Quite so, Doctor Cole," agreed the inspector going towards the door. "I must admit the suggestion of a third robbery being attempted at Melton Grange did seem rather unlikely. But in the circumstances, I thought it best to investigate."

"Of course. I shall arrange for the necessary repairs as soon as possible, so that the drama festival can continue. Fortunately, nothing appears to be badly damaged."

"Thank goodness that's over," breathed Lynsey, once the men had departed. "I was beginning to think you'd all done something really terrible."

"No," said Oliver seriously, remembering the two voices they had heard the night before. "Not us, Lynsey."

It was what Lynsey called "a muddly sort of morning". Rehearsals were out of the question, because nobody could get into any of the rooms around the Great Hall, and the whole of Melton Grange seemed to be crowded with drama groups trying to find somewhere to go.

"Let's take a look and see if anyone's started on the Great Hall," suggested Oliver, trying to think of some way to pass the time.

But, not surprisingly, the doors were still locked, and there was another blackboard with the words "DANGER. KEEP OUT." scrawled on it. So, they went out of the building and round to the side entrance, half-walking, half-creeping along the corridor which led alongside the cloakroom.

"See anything, Ollie?" asked Scott, trying to nudge him out of the way so that he could peer through the wide chink in the doorway.

"Wow!" He gave a low whistle. "Those swords and things are gi-normous, aren't they?"

"And the wooden shield bit that was in the middle!" added Rachel. "Must be nearly twice as big as a dustbin lid!"

"All the swords were wedged into that," put in Tina. "Once that fell, it brought the whole lot down with it!"

"Amazing none of them got broken," remarked Scott once they were outside again. "Trouble is, we can't very well go nosing around in the rest of the lobbies for any clues about the boss with a red tie, just yet, can we?"

"Not until that display is mended," Jason agreed soberly.

"Hey, Rachel! Oliver!" somebody called, and they turned round to see Tony calling across to them. "How do you fancy listening to Madame Helga going on about voice-work in the library?"

"Not much!" Rachel grinned back, but she knew Lynsey would start asking questions if they didn't go. "Is it going to last long, do you know?"

Tony shrugged. "I think it's only to keep everyone out of the way while the Great Hall starts getting back to normal! Save you some seats in the front row, shall I?"

"Thanks," said Rachel tartly. "I'll look forward to that!"

"Mask-making in the school craft room this afternoon!" Mark added teasingly. "Remember to give Betty a clap every time she pauses for breath, and it will be just like going to the dentist. You know, a bit of a drag, but not really as bad as you expected!"

"Okay, then!" retorted Scott with some spirit. "You can sit in the front row!"

He went follow them into the corridor, ready to shout out something else. But a young, thin-faced man in faded overalls was coming in the opposite direction, carrying a long ladder with some difficulty.

"Can't you see I'm waiting to come in?" he snarled at Scott. "You kids should be out of here by now, not hanging around making nuisances of yourself!" He sauntered off in the direction of the Great Hall.

Tina turned to Scott. She thought she had never seen him look quite so serious.

"What's the matter, Scott?"

"I — don't know," he admitted. "There's something I remembered, then forgot. You know, one of those things that comes into your head for a second, then it goes."

Rachel was about to say he was sounding more like Jason every day. But Madame Helga was watching, so she looked around for somewhere to sit, instead. There was hardly any room to move, with all the chairs grouped awkwardly around the bookcases and the display cabinets so that everyone could get in.

"Come along, find a seat, dear!" cooed Madame Helga. Rachel didn't know it, but the lady had taken quite a fancy to her long hair and blue eyes, privately considering that she was wasting her time at Studio Workshop. "Sit next to my Amanda, that's right."

She beamed approvingly, quite content to see Scott and Jason squeezing in at the back of the room.

"You two can come out and read something for me, can't you? It's only a short piece, just to see how you get on."

Tina was getting worried. Scott seemed pale and dazed, and she could see him fingering the bruise on his forehead.

"And we'll have Mark reading the narrator's part!" Madame Helga prattled on, almost lugging him out of the audience. From the look on his face, it was clear he had been planning to while away a lazy half-hour, thinking about nothing in particular, and Rachel felt quite sorry for him. With so many people in the library, it was already uncomfortably warm and stuffy.

"Napoleon was getting his fleet ready for the battle of Trafalgar. . . "

100

"Your turn to be Napoleon, dear," said Madame Helga, giving Jason an encouraging push.

"At zis date, we shall sail on ze first tide, my brave admiral!" Accents had never been Jason's strong point, but he was doing his best. "What have you to say?"

"Go on, Scott," Mark hissed, seeing him hesitate. "That's where you come in."

"No. wait a moment!" Madame Helga consulted her script. "Did Napoleon say 'At this date we shall sail on the first tide,' or 'At this state we shall sail on the first side'? You're confusing your fellow actors, dear!"

There was a ripple of amusement and Jason went red, glad that Lynsey wasn't there to see his discomfort. Madame Helga was right, he knew, but it was impossible to think clearly that morning, and he was beginning to feel niggly and impatient with himself.

Scotty wasn't much help, either, he thought. He could see him gazing all round the walls, scratching his forehead, not even following his script. And if he missed the cue for the Admiral again, Madame Helga would think it was all his fault and start picking holes in his French accent, again...

"Jason!" exclaimed Madame Helga, making him look up sharply. "Jason, that was your introduction which Mark just read. Wake up, now!"

"Er, yes. Sorry..." Scotty was mouthing something at him, putting his hand to his head again, and trying to point at the door. Some of the Langham Theatre School near the front thought he was making fun of Madame Helga, and started to giggle.

"Just a little slower," prompted Madame Helga. "And lift your head, so that we can hear all the words, nice and clear."

By now Jason was desperate, so he did the first thing he could think of. He turned over two pages of the script at once, throwing both Mark and Madame Helga into complete confusion, and succeeded in dropping the whole lot of papers on the floor.

"I think we'll try somebody else," announced Madame Helga, leaving Jason and Scott to pick everything up. "What about some people from the Elmfield Drama Group this time?"

"What's the idea, Scotty?" growled Jason, annoyed at all the giggling which was still going on. "First you're standing there like a stuffed dummy saying nothing, then you start acting like a prize twit. I could crown you, honestly, I could!"

"Listen, I would've crowned myself, if I hadn't just thought of what I was trying to remember," He let some of the papers float towards the big fireplace, so that they had to go and rescue them, as far from Madame Helga and the audience as they dared go.

"You know the workman, the one going into the Great Hall?"

"Yes, 'course I do! What about him?"

"He's got a bump on his head, Jason. A great, big, wicked bump on his head, after creeping around between the lobbies last night."

Sixteen

It was a squash inside Kate's cleaning lobby, with everyone wanting to look down into the Great Hall at the same time.

"I'm telling you, that man's got a bump on his head!" Scott kept saying.

Oliver was almost convinced. But not quite.

"We heard those two crooks saying they were on the look-out for a boss with a red tie, right?"

"Quiet, Ollie," ordered Matthew, flapping a hand at him. "Look, Mabel's coming in with the tea trolley."

"Like a cup of tea?" Mabel called up to him. The man was too far away to catch what he said, but Mabel called out again.

"Come and help yourself to milk and sugar, then. I'll take the trolley back in a minute."

"He's coming down, right now, Matthew," breathed Oliver. "Ever seen him before?"

"No, can't say I have. Scotty's right about the bump, though. You can see him wincing every time he goes to put his cap straight, and I think there's quite a bruise, as well."

"That's still no proof that he's one of the man we heard talking about the Lady Elizabeth chalice," said Oliver, kneeling back after a while. "Neither of them would be messing around, putting swords back on a wall, would they?"

"That could be a cover-up," said Matthew thoughtfully. "It might even be the reason why that display came down in the first place, to give somebody a good excuse to be here."

"You mean," spluttered Jason, "it was done on purpose? But Doctor Cole said it was an accident! He said he was calling in the experts!"

"Couldn't we get Doctor Cole to check on that workman?" Rachel suggested, once they'd all had a chance to think. "Without going into any details, I mean?"

Matthew sighed, clutching at his mop of red hair.

"I'd like to keep the Doc out of this, if we can. He's the one who got permission from the Head for me to do the project on the Lady Elizabeth chalice. He even lent me his camera to take some of the photographs. If anyone finds out I'm here, they might think he had something to do with it."

"And if that guy is one of the crooks trying to get the Lady Elizabeth chalice," added Oliver, "he could easily warn the other one, the man who got this Shorty to pinch it and put the blame on Matthew!"

Scott was bitterly disappointed. He had visualized police cars racing to Melton Grange, sirens blaring, ready to arrest the workman and get him to tell them the name of the other man. Even then the Lady Elizabeth chalice would still be missing, hidden away in the care of the boss with the red tie.

The boss with the red tie. Scott was thinking about him all through John Turner's mask-making session.

"You can try using paper plates, empty cereal packets, cardboard boxes," he was telling everyone grouped around the biggest table in the Melton Grange craft room. "The idea is to try and create a character which you could act later on."

Scott said nothing, but his hands worked on, drawing and painting, then adding a splodgy nose, false eyebrows and thick, black wool for hair. It gave him some satisfaction to look straight into the hard, staring eyes he had imagined, and see the cruel mouth, thin and unsmiling.

"Now that's what I call a real character, Scott," smiled John Turner, looking over his shoulder. "Definitely a front-runner for the part of the villain!"

"It's the boss!" announced Scott on the spur of the moment, reaching for the paint pots. "The boss with the red tie!"

John turner laughed out loud. "The boss with the red tie?" he gurgled. "Sounds like something out of a gangster movie!"

Scott wasn't sure about that, but he was both pleased and flattered by all the attention he was suddenly getting. He put the mask up to his face, turning his head this way and that, and waggling his hands, making everyone look up and grin at him.

"You ought to wear that thing going downstairs!" Oliver told him. "Might make that workman fall off his ladder!"

"Well, I wouldn't fall over myself to go and pick him up!" said Stacy from Mainline Players, overhearing the last remark. "Some of us only wanted a close look at the swords and everything – you know, before they go back on the wall. He nearly bit our heads off!"

"Didn't say anything to that Madame Helga and Fellowes, though," added Tony indignantly. "Walked in as if they were in charge of the whole operation, they did."

"Sounds as if they know the workman, then," Oliver commented, making an effort to keep his voice steady. All this sounded very suspicious, and he meant to find out as much as he could.

Scott had made up his mind to wear his "boss mask", as he called it, and go into the Great Hall – "just to see if there's anything else we can find out," he said. Jason and Oliver thought that was a good idea.

"If anyone asks, we want to see the swords," he added.

Oliver opened the door, surprised to find the hall quite deserted.

All the swords and the centre-piece had now been lifted on to the stage. But, apart from the gaping hole where the display had been and the workman's ladder still propped up against the wall, nothing much seemed to have been done.

"Not many scratches on the floor, either," Jason commented, searching around for any signs of damage where the swords had fallen. "Strange, that. And, everything that was on the wall is still in one piece."

"Maybe the stuff didn't fall down, then," mused Oliver, scuffing the wooden blocks with the toe of his shoe. "Maybe someone only pretended that's what happened, just to get the chance of putting it back again. . . "

A shrill, strangled little scream reached Scott's ears, and he whirled round, trying to squint through the pin-pricks he had made in the eyes. Suddenly, there was the sound of a smothered giggle, with somebody else trying hard not to laugh.

"Nice try, Scotty!" Mark's voice rang out. "Now, put your funny face back on!"

Scott pulled off the mask, almost breaking the elastic in the process.

"You might have told me it was only the Langham lot," he accused Oliver, annoyed at the thought of everyone enjoying a joke, except him. "Who banged open the door like that? And who screamed?"

"Me," Lynette confessed rather sheepishly. "Sorry if I scared you."

"We were meant to be keeping an eye on the place, while Betty went off to see where that workman had gone," Mark explained with a grin. "She's making a real fuss over these swords, you know."

"Still, she did manage to wangle a room for us so that we could do an extra rehearsal for our production, Mark," said Lynette. "We'd only have been stuck in the craft room making masks, otherwise."

"That's what we've been doing," Rachel reminded her tartly. Lynette gave her a friendly push.

"Don't get upset, Rachel. Look, we're at stage school practically every day of the week. Stands to reason we've done a load of things that you're still learning about."

"And it wasn't much fun standing and listening to a lecture on a load of old swords for half an hour, either," grumbled Amanda. "Trust Betty to make the most of her big moment!"

"She seems to know a lot about that stuff at Melton Grange," commented Scott, becoming suspicious again. Absent-mindedly, he twanged the elastic on the back of his mask, and it gave him another idea to try.

"When Madame Helga was talking to you, about the swords and everything, was Fellowes there as well? And the workman?"

Mark glanced at Lynette and Amanda before he answered.

"Yes. Fellowes kept chipping in with some facts of his own, and you could see the workman was getting a bit hot under the collar. I think he wanted to get on with the job. Why d'you ask, Scotty?"

Scott took a deep breath, his eyes fixed still on the mask. Jason could guess what was coming next.

"I was just wondering. Did you hear them mention the boss?"

"They didn't just mention the boss," said Lynette with a groan, "they went on about it for nearly half an hour. Don't say you're interested, as well."

"Doesn't look all the special," continued Mark, strolling

107

towards the deserted stage. "More or less a wooden shield thing with a coat of arms painted on. Tons bigger than you'd expect, though."

The disbelief showed clearly in their faces as they gathered in front of the stage, following the direction of Jason's pointing finger.

"That — that round wooden thing that all the swords fit into?" he faltered. "That's the boss?"

"So Betty and Fellowes told us. Over two hundred years old, they said."

"Just imagine, a thing like that being called a boss," Amanda started giggling helplessly. "You'd never have thought it, would you?"

Seventeen

When Scott and Jason said they wanted to know about the swords, Madame Helga was delighted. She always enjoyed having an audience.

"Now, these are ceremonial swords, not the ones used for combat. They're made of Welsh steel, but the enamel work on this hilt was probably done by — "

"What about the boss, Madame Helga?" Scott broke in eagerly. "How does that hold all the swords in place?"

"Well, with this one, there are these little clamps which fix into a bracket on the wall." She heaved it towards her with some difficulty, so that the boys could see the back. "Other bosses have long pegs or screws which go right through the wall, held tight by a wedge at the other side. Rather like an ordinary nut and bolt, but much longer."

"What about the front?" Jason asked.

"Well, that's where all the decoration is, of course. This has a coat of arms, but it could be a shield, a family motto, or — "

"Er — what about something like a red tie?" Scott interrupted again, the words coming out in a rush. Madame Helga seemed puzzled, but then her marshmallow face cleared.

"You've been talking to Reginald — I mean, Fellowes — haven't you? He said he'd heard someone mentioning a boss with a red tie. All I could think of was a red ribbon, tied in a bow, or a red knot on a shield, but there's nothing like that at Melton Grange, I'm afraid."

"Now," she continued happily, "if you look at the carving around the edge — "

But Jason and Scott were no longer listening. Instead, they glanced at each other across Madame Helga's froth of pink-rinsed hair, and sighed.

Not that Madame Helga noticed. And she was still talking when she met Lynsey in the dining hall later on.

"Do you know, those boys stood listening to every word I said. So interested and willing to learn."

"Gave us some great ideas for props and scenery, Lynsey," announced Scott, seeing the somewhat distant smile on her pretty face. "You wait till we get back to Dreyton Manor."

"Ah, yes. Your new arts centre, Lynsey," cooed Madame Helga, taking her arm. "You must come over to my table and tell me all about it."

Scott and Jason glanced at each other again, grinning this time. Madame Helga might be a real pain, but her flair for non-stop chatter certainly had its uses.

"Makes it easier for us to get away without Lynsey asking any awkward questions," Oliver agreed.

"Fancy the boss being a thing on the wall," groaned Rachel, gulping down the last of her coffee. "We've been right mutts, all along!"

"Well, we're getting a bit closer now," Oliver glanced around, making sure that everyone else was busy, chatting and eating. The last day of the drama festival, when each group would be staging their own productions, was fast approaching, and everyone was looking forward to it. There was too much noise and too much excitement for anyone to notice one table slowly clearing.

"You finished early!" commented Matthew, opening the door at the agreed two knocks. "What's up now?"

"Plenty!" exclaimed Jason, handing over a ham sandwich and some biscuits and cheese. "So, just listen, and don't ask any questions until we've finished. OK?"

110

Rachel, Tina and Oliver had not yet heard what Madame Helga said about the boss and the red tie, so they were just as interested as Matthew.

"How come there's always a snag?" complained Oliver, when Jason had finished. "You'd think Madame Helga would know if there was a boss with a red tie, wouldn't you?"

"Hang on a sec. . ." Matthew broke in. "That workman, or whoever he is. . . Suppose he took that boss off the wall, thinking the Lady Elizabeth chalice was hidden behind it?"

"Of course!" Oliver's brown eyes gleamed. "Why else were those crooks creeping around between the lobbies? They even said they had to find the boss, didn't they? Now, we know what they meant!"

"The peep-holes that look out into the Great Hall. . ." said Jason, beginning to understand. "One of those could be near the boss where Shorty hid the chalice. Madame Helga said that some bosses had long wooden pegs which went right through the wall, with a wooden wedge at the other side."

"It'll be quicker if we search through the rafters in twos," Oliver decided at last, pulling his bed out from the wall, ready to drag the box of stage equipment off the loose floorboard. "Matt can come with me, and you go in the opposite direction with Jason, Scotty!"

"What about me and Tina?" demanded Rachel.

"You two can search all the lobbies leading off the stairs," ordered Oliver, lifting up the floorboard with Jason's help. "Take the torches again — and don't forget, it's the side facing the Great Hall that we're interested in!"

Just then there was a sharp rap at the door, making them all jump.

"Scott!" a familiar voice called, followed by another knock. "Scott, are you up here?"

"That's John Turner," whispered Jason. "What does he want?"

They all kept quiet, leaving Scott to go and lift the latch, poking his head around the door.

"I – I was just going to have a shower," he explained.

"So that's why you vanished at the speed of light. Look, any chance of you coming down to the Great Hall when you've finished? I'd like to work through the demo on sound effects that we talked about."

"No need to look so worried," the man laughed, unaware of the consternation his words were causing, "It's only going to be a short session, before the dress rehearsals start. Can you bring your gear downstairs in about half an hour?"

"OK, then," Scott agreed, his heart sinking. Of all the times to get roped in for something like this, he told himself.

"You'd better go with him, Jason," said Oliver, and Matthew nodded in agreement. "That way, you can keep together and carry on with the search as soon as John Turner's finished."

"You'll probably think up a good excuse to get away quickly," added Matthew, trying to keep their spirits up.

It seemed very unlikely. John turner wanted to inspect all the wiring and each cassette recorder, as well as every tape and microphone they had brought with them. Lynsey was there, too, telling him all about the sound effects Scott had done for *The Merrie Devil*, and he had to hear those, as well.

"Great idea to have two tapes playing at the same time!" he exclaimed, enjoying a series of blood-curdling moans and groans for the scene in the haunted Whispering Chamber. "Does it make any difference where you put the recorders?"

And so it went on. Questions about volume of sound,

fast rewinds, double tracking, stand microphones.

"Poor old Scotty," said Rachel, looking down into the Great Hall from the Green Suite storeroom. "Doesn't look very happy, does he?"

"Nor does Jason," added Tina, ready to slide the wood back into place. "Rachel..."

"Yes?"

"This skirting board... Could there be more than one piece that slides back? A piece behind one of the bosses, like Jason said?"

"Only one way to find out," Rachel sighed, getting ready to haul a row of cartons and bundles out of the way.

It was quite a while before they found what they were looking for – a length of steel with a handle in the middle, a bit like the lid of a casserole dish. It was very stiff, and little showers of rust spurted out whenever they managed to move it.

"Can't have been shifted for years!" puffed Rachel, trying to bang it further along with the palm of her hand. "But you're right, Tina," she added, squinting through the space she had made. "I can see a great big wedge-thing over the end of a huge wooden peg! It must be one of the bosses!"

She and Tina were still trying to move it further along when the hatch door clicked open and Matthew and Oliver squeezed inside. They were both very dirty and untidy.

"We seem to be getting nowhere," Oliver complained, brushing down the sleeves of his sweatshirt. "No sign of any boss with a red tie, either."

"Well, at least we've got a boss," declared Rachel, peering through the gap again. "Take a look, Ollie!"

Rachel and Tina were glad to see the boys interested in their find, but that didn't help when it came to sliding back the length of steel. In the end, after lots more tugging and pulling, they gave up.

"Can't be where Shorty hid the Lady Elizabeth chalice," announced Oliver, examining the grazed knuckles of one hand. "It'd take a superman to move that thing!"

"Must be something like it, though," said Matthew. "And Shorty marked it with a red tie, for those two men to find. The thing is, what sort of tie did he mean?"

He clutched at his red hair, the same as he always did when he was trying to work something out. Tina gave a gasp of horror.

"What have you done to your hand, Matthew! It's bleeding!"

"Eh?" He glanced down quickly and laughed. "No, I'm OK. This is the result of trying to crash into a lobby with a load of paint stacked up against the hatch door. I must have caught my hand on a lid, or something."

"Looks pretty gruesome, though, doesn't it?" he went on, trying to wipe it off with his handkerchief. "Can't remember the last time there was painting being done at Melton Grange, either."

"But that paint's wet," Oliver pointed out. "So somebody's had the lid off since then."

Rachel had been listening carefully to all this. Now, she grabbed Matthew's hand and sniffed.

"Smells more like greasepaint than anything else," she said at last, wrinkling up her nose. "Reminds me of Madame Helga!"

"Or something that Scott's used when he's been making up props or scenery with Jason," added Tina. "More of a dye..."

"A red dye..." said Oliver slowly, looking at Matthew's hand. "Are you all thinking what I'm thinking?"

"Remember Madame Helga going on at Jason about his phoney French accent?" cried Rachel, jabbing a finger in her excitement. "About saying this state, when he meant this date? And first side, instead of first tide?"

"Now we've got a red dye, instead of red tie," finished Tina. "Do you know which lobby it was, Matthew?"

"I – I think so!" He looked around at their beaming faces, hope shining in his eyes. "Yes! Yes, of course, I do!"

"OK, so what are you waiting for?" said Oliver, wishing he could start cheering. "That's where we'll find the boss, with the Lady Elizabeth chalice hidden behind it."

There was a polite cough, and the sound of a key grating in a lock.

"Pity to interrupt such an interesting conversation," purred a smooth voice.

The figure came closer towards them, cruel eyes staring unblinkingly, lips pressed together in a thin line.

"Surely you recognize me?" Now Oliver could see why the voice sounded strangely muffled.

"Scotty's mask!" he choked. "The boss with the red tie!"

"Exactly! And now, you and your friends are going to show me precisely where the Lady Elizabeth chalice has been left for me to collect. Start leading the way!"

Eighteen

Oliver could see there was no escape.

Before, they had all laughed at Scott's comical mask of the "boss with the red tie". Now, it made Tina want to scream out loud, the horrible way the eyes seemed to stare at her, and the sneer of the cruel lips.

"Ginger-nut can lead the way, I think!" came the strange, muffled voice again, grabbing Matthew by the shoulder. "And I'm warning you, Fingers is right outside. One false move, and he'll be down on you like a ton of bricks."

"Let Rachel and Tina get behind him," said Oliver. The man in the mask did not answer, just gave a curt nod and waved them through the hatch door.

"Now you," he told Oliver gruffly, giving him a push. "Go on, get moving! And don't turn round!"

Matthew led the way as slowly as he dared, hoping that Scott and Jason had left the Great Hall by now. With any luck, they could soon be returning to their room, lifting up the loose floorboard and lowering themselves down among the old rafters.

Would they be able to get away and fetch help, send for the police and everything? There was a chance, thought Matthew, his heart beginning to beat more quickly.

"Come on, come on!" growled the voice at the back, as Matthew stumbled among the rafters, through to the hatch door of the next lobby. "I haven't got all night."

"He might not be able to remember where it is," protested Oliver, and got a swift, vicious cuff across the back of his head.

"He remembers, all right! I heard him say so!"

116

"I think it's the hatch door just ahead," Matthew said bleakly.

"Hey, Fingers!" the man called over his shoulder into the shadows behind him, as Matthew reached out a hand to pull open the hatch door. "On guard, over here!"

"Quite a cosy little party we're having, isn't it?" he went on, flashing a torch all around the crowded little lobby. "And don't put that light on," he rapped out at Oliver. "Get over here and let's see the boss."

The splashes of red dye on the floor and spattered on an old-fashioned wooden crate showed that there was no mistake. They all knew what was hidden behind it, even before the man heaved it aside to reveal the long, iron panel.

"Pull it back!" the man ordered. "No, not you!" he snapped at Oliver. "Let Ginger-nut do it!"

In silence they watched Matthew kneel down and reach for the handle on the panel. The piece of iron moved smoothly to one side, hardly making a sound.

"This is it, Fingers," the man muttered, half to himself. "This is it!"

Tina and Rachel held tightly to each other, hardly able to look. The wooden peg and the wedge at the back of the boss were both thick with soot and dust, setting off the sheen on a piece of black velvet.

"Open it!" barked the man, giving Matthew a kick to show he meant business. "Go on, let's all see what's inside."

He towered over Matthew, standing there until he had unwrapped the velvet, letting it fall on to the bare floorboards.

The chalice was even more beautiful than it had appeared in the photographs. All the engravings stood out clearly in the soft light, which also lent a mellow glow to the gold and picked out the glint of the precious stones set into the handles.

"Know how much that's worth?" crowed the man, kicking Matthew again. "Five times more than this place and everything inside it. Tomorrow there'll be a dozen people, each of them ready to pay any price I like to ask."

"Ah, Fingers!" he cried, as the hatch door opened again. "Come on in. You've met this lot, I believe."

"Yeah..." Oliver could see Fingers rubbing the bump on his head. "Yeah, I've met 'em, guv. And I'm only sorry I nabbed the wrong one in the library."

"Oh, all is forgiven, Fingers," the man declared, wrapping the chalice almost nonchalantly in the piece of velvet. "We've got the chalice now. Quite a clever hiding place Shorty found."

"Too clever for you!" Oliver could not help bursting out. He ducked, thinking he would receive another blow. But the man threw back his head, laughing behind the mask like some sort of nightmarish monster on a ghost train.

"That remark shows that you do not know just how clever I have been. I saw to it that your friend's fingerprints are on all the hatch doors, to say nothing of the handle on the back of the boss. The blame will still be on him."

"And don't waste time telling me all that you plan to say to the police," he went on, with an airy wave of his hand. "The boy knows as well as I that he cannot stay at Melton Grange as a suspected thief. How can his innocence be proved, now?"

Almost mechanically, Matthew reached out to slide the iron panel back into place, turning his head away to hide his unhappiness. The splashes of red dye on his hands were still there. He could just pick them out in a faint glimmer of light coming from the Great Hall below.

He gave a loud gulp, so that he knew Oliver and Rachel

would look at him, beginning to edge away from the boss.

"That's Scotty's mask!" Oliver shouted accusingly. "You pinched that from our room!"

"You've been here at Melton Grange the whole time, haven't you?" Rachel challenged him bravely, just as he was about to strike Oliver again. "We know! We heard you telling Fingers about the kids from Studio Workshop!"

Oliver could see Matthew was only inches away from the wooden handle now, so he began tackling the man again. Anything, he told himself, to stop him from looking round to see what Matt was doing.

"And how come you know your way around Melton Grange so well? How did Fingers get in, pretending to mend a display which he'd taken down off the wall?"

"And, that's why. . ." Tina faltered, swallowing hard and pointing at the mask. "That's why. . ."

"Go on!" came the man's sneering voice, cradling the black velvet parcel to his chest. "You're doing so well, don't let me stop you!"

"That's why nothing got broken! That's why the floor wasn't scratched! And that's why you're afraid to take off the mask and face us properly!"

"Why, you little – " began Fingers, making a grab at Tina. She tried to dodge out of his way, falling over a pile of old books, but he hauled her to her feet again.

"Scotty!" Matthew yelled down into the Great Hall. "Jason!" But his cries were completely drowned out by a series of low, wailing moans, rising up to a scream then plunging to a tormented whisper.

"Wh – what's that, guv?" stammered Fingers, loosening his hold on Tina.

Behind the mask, the man gave a loud exclamation of impatience, cutting out a few of the words which floated into the tiny lobby.

... such dread and such fear
Shall fear the hearts of those who draw near...
For, naught but the brave can dare win the day,
The ghosts of Dreyton to send far away!

"G-ghosts?" repeated Fingers, the moment the word was mentioned. "G-ghosts?"

"Quite, you fool. It's only a play in this stupid drama festival."

"Scotty!" Matthew seized the chance to start yelling again. "Scotty, we're up here! Jason!"

"You can save your breath!" The man slammed across the piece of wood so hard that Matthew caught his hand inside, crying out in pain. "By the time anybody gets up here, we'll be gone and the Lady Elizabeth chalice with us. Such a shame your friends chose this very evening to do their sound recordings, isn't it?"

The two men walked to the door, Fingers swinging some keys on a chain.

"Lock us in," said Oliver, "and we'll get through the hatch doors, through to the rafters again."

"You'll be lucky," cackled Fingers. "'Cos I've wedged 'em tight shut, see? Like the guv'nor says, you don't know how clever he is."

"But bang and shout on the doors by all means," said the masked man airily. "I have a very fast car waiting downstairs. Ten minutes or so should be more than enough for a getaway. And that's not counting the time it's going to take for you to spin your jolly little tale and summon our friend, Inspector Drew."

"You – you won't get away with it!" cried Matthew desperately. "Th – those wails, the creepy voice and everything... it – it's all part of a curse on anyone who

120

tries stealing the Lady Elizabeth chalice. I – I thought it was only a story when I read it, but – "

"A – a curse?" They could see Fingers hesitating, even backing away a little.

"Oh, come along, you great idiot!" exclaimed the man in the mask, pulling at the door. "There's nothing to stop us now!"

Without any warning, the door opened wide and the little room flooded with light.

"That's where you're wrong," somebody proclaimed loudly, "Completely wrong."

Everyone else was still blinking, unable to see very much except a tall, dark shadow looming in the doorway, a shadow which only Matthew seemed to recognize, his lips parting in a cry of disbelief.

"No! No, it – it can't be! How did you get here? I thought I'd never see you again!"

Nineteen

Although Matthew had despaired of anyone in the Great Hall hearing him, somebody had. Lynsey's sharp ears had caught his cries, but she was too far away to see anything more than a quick glimpse of his red hair.

"Well, I think we've got more than enough here for a first class demonstration," John Turner was telling Scott and Jason. "And your *Merrie Devil* really shows how much a production can depend on sound effects. Eh, Lynsey?"

"Lynsey?" he said again, surprised at her sudden lack of interest.

"No, there can't be..." she muttered to herself. "Not somebody else like Scott, crawling around where he shouldn't...' red hair, and everything..."

Scott saw her looking up at a display on the wall, and he guessed what had happened.

"Matthew!" he yelled, trying unsuccessfully to escape a length of wire with a microphone at one end. "Matthew, hold on!"

"Come on, Jason!" he shouted, sprinting towards the swing doors, stuffing the wire in his pockets. "Matt's in a fix!"

Together, the boys raced to the service lift, slamming the door shut. They had no idea which lobby Matthew was in, but Scott guessed it must be on the opposite side of the building to their room.

"Along this corridor," he panted to Jason, trying to stop the wire trailing out of his pocket at the same time. "It must lead to another landing."

They kept running, getting more and more out of breath, but were brought up suddenly by a ruthless voice below them, down a short flight of stairs:

"There's nothing you can do, any of you! Nobody's going to make me hand over the Lady Elizabeth chalice!"

One of the doors swung open. Jason and Scott stood quite still. A strange figure was backing out, something wrapped in black velvet clutched to his chest, and a mask covering his face.

"Come on, Fingers! Time we were going!"

"Don't be a fool!" To their complete amazement, it was Fellowes surging forward, trying to grab the man's sleeve. He was shrugged off so fiercely, that he fell to the ground with a thud.

"Anyone else like to try and stop me?" sneered the voice behind the mask, backing further out of the door.

It was only a wild shot, but Scott knew he had to take it, fumbling frantically to pull the wire from his pocket. The microphone at one end gave it weight as he threw it down the last three or four stairs, landing at the heels of the masked man with a bang.

The man whirled round at once, so quickly that one foot became caught up in the wire, and he tried to kick it away.

"Don't just stand there, Fingers!" he cried in desperation. "Do something!"

Fingers dashed forward. The moment he turned his back, Matthew and Jason threw themselves at him, Matthew diving for his ankles.

"An excellent rugby tackle!" somebody called. "Well done, my boy!"

Seeing Fingers out of action made the masked man more desperate. Still kicking at the wire round his feet, he tried rushing downstairs. But Lynsey and John Turner were already there, facing him.

"Out of my way!" he thundered, aiming a kick at them. "Out of my way!"

Bravely, John Turner put his foot on the bottom stair, and the masked man made the mistake of kicking out for the last time. Down he fell, Scott's wire curled around one leg. And from the piece of black velvet the Lady Elizabeth chalice rolled on to the floor, gleaming softly.

The fall had also broken the mask, making the hideous face loll to one side of the head in a way that gave Rachel the shivers.

"Take it off!" she screamed. "Take the mask off!"

It was Jason who bent over and slid the elastic over the top of the man's head, now thrown back in pain.

"Doctor Cole," breathed Oliver, his brown eyes widening. "It – it's Doctor Cole."

The silence which followed was broken by a chorus of sirens outside.

"That will be the Police, sir," announced Fellowes, straightening up with as much dignity as he could muster. "I telephoned Inspector Drew immediately after I had spoken to you."

"Yes! Yes, of course, Fellowes! I do not think Cole and his companion will give us any more trouble."

"And now, sir," said Matthew, taking the distinguished-looking grey-haired man by the arm, "I'd like you to meet my friends from Studio Workshop. This is Oliver. And, this," he told Oliver, "is my headmaster, Professor James."

As Tina said afterwards, everything made sense, once you thought about it. Doctor Cole getting Matthew interested in the chalice to begin with, his copies of the photographs which they had found, and how he had known about Studio Workshop being at Melton Grange.

"And it explains how Fingers could show his face in the Great Hall, after the sword display came down from the wall." said Oliver, taking a chocolate eclair from the cake stand which Mabel offered him.

They were all having what Professor James called "a late coffee break" in his study, and enjoying it very much.

"Weren't you telling me, it was that which made you suspicious, Fellowes?" he said.

"I have had my suspicions all along, Headmaster. When I reported the theft of the chalice to the police, I had no idea Matthew Forrest would be accused. The whole idea was absurd."

"And that's why you wanted to keep the whole business as quiet as you could?" Lynsey enquired gently.

"Quite so, Miss Ronald," Fellowes nodded, lowering his cup. "But I could hardly have foreseen another young man with red hair coming to Melton Grange for the drama festival."

"Now you know why I wanted you to return home," he said, turning to Scott. "When you were attacked in the library, I knew that Forrest had been the victim of a criminal plot, and I feared for your safety."

"No wonder you got into a state when we asked you about the boss," grinned Scott.

"Yes, and when the boss and those swords were taken down, Doctor Cole said he heard a crash. That's when I knew for certain that he was the person behind the robbery."

"But we still had no idea where the Lady Elizabeth chalice had been hidden," Inspector Drew added. "Thank goodness you lot solved that part of the mystery for us."

"Yes, they're a great bunch," Matthew agreed, smiling. "I could never have managed without them, I know that!"

"And how do you feel about returning to school on Monday, Forrest?" asked the headmaster. "Melton Grange is relying on you to select a first class rugby fifteen in time for the new season."

"I'll look forward to that, sir," said Matthew. "But there happens to be another clever character that I have to see, first." He grinned quickly in Oliver's direction. "John Gabriel the blacksmith, otherwise known as The Merrie Devil of Dreyton."

It was difficult to get through the dress rehearsals once the news got round Melton Grange, the robbery and how they had tracked down the boss and the Lady Elizabeth chalice.

Everywhere they went, people from the other groups kept coming up and asking questions, some even wanting to take photographs and exchange names and addresses.

"I'll write and send you tickets for our next production," Mark told them. "Mind you, it won't have any of your super sound effects. But none of us can be good at everything, can we?"

"No," sighed Tina, watching the Langham chorus line, perfectly in step under the watchful eye of Madame Helga. "No, we can't be good at everything! Only, some of us are good at more things than others!"

"You're still coming in at least half a beat too slow, Lynette!" cried Madame Helga. "Amanda missed her first quarter-turn, and as for Joanne – "

"No mistaking a production when Betty's in charge, eh?" Mark commented jokingly. "She knows what she wants, that's the trouble."

"Yes," Tina agreed, "and she knows what she's talking about."

Whether Lynette got her timing right, or if Amanda managed the vexed quarter-turn, Tina never did find out. As far as she was concerned, The Langham Theatre School revue was as polished and as well-produced on stage as the day she had first seen it being rehearsed.

"Mark's a great compère, isn't he?" cried Rachel, joining in the clapping and the cheering. "We'll have to try some variety stuff when we get back home."

"That's after practising some of the mime we saw Mainline Players doing," Oliver reminded her. "And you've got that script for a puppet show from Picton Youth Drama."

"Just as long as you give a good performance of *The Merrie Devil* tomorrow afternoon," warned Lynsey. "I don't want anyone treading on my toes at the farewell party because my group's put them through an hour of misery!"

Oliver had also wondered if Studio Workshop's production would be as good as everyone else's at the festival. Helping Matthew find that Lady Elizabeth chalice had taken up a lot of their time, when they could have been brushing up their lines.

But the warm burst of applause which broke out when the curtain went up in the Great Hall convinced him that none of them need have worried.

The cheers for John Gabriel . . . the gasps of delight when Tina as his magical servant Firefly leapt about on stage, leading the demons to haunt the Whispering Chamber. . . the hisses and boos for the villain, Lord Cuthbert — each response came at exactly the right moment.

Would poor Edwin survive the night and win the hand of Mathilda, the miller's daughter? Or — could it be Lord Cuthbert who would stand the test set by Squire Melrose of Dreyton?

And when Rachel appeared in her wedding dress as Mathilda, with Scott as her proud bridegroom, Edwin, the applause began again.

"But were they cheering us, or the play?" Oliver wanted to know, as they stood together after the final curtain. "I never thought Fellowes was going to stop clapping."

There were still more cheers and more clapping when Oliver led his friends out in front of the curtain. In the end, Professor James had to come up on to the stage, holding up both hands for the audience to be quiet.

None of them really remembered what he said, except that Lynsey smiled and looked proud, and people still kept clapping, with Fellows and Madame Helga calling out "Hear, hear!" almost every time Professor James said something about Studio Workshop.

Madame Helga and Fellowes were at the farewell party, too, dazzling everyone with their ballroom dancing.

"Funny to think about it, really," Matthew pondered, helping Kate to hand round the glasses of cola and lemonade. "Just over a week ago, I was looking forward to half term. Then it seemed like I'd be expelled. And now, the Head is going around telling everyone that I'm some sort of hero."

"Like playing a part in our play," put in Jason thoughtfully. "You know, Scotty's the good guy, I'm the baddie, Ollie's the hero, Ratchet's the leading lady..."

"And Tina's the bit of magic that makes everything come right in the end," grinned Matthew, taking her hand. "Come on, Firefly!"

It was clear that he felt like dancing.